HAPPY HOUR FOOLS

Libby Belle

Pure Luck
Press

Happy Hour Fools
Stories by Libby Belle

Published by Pure Luck Press
LibbyBelle.com
Austin, Texas

ISBN02: 978-0-9985165-5-4 (Ebook)
ISBN: 978-0-9985165-4-7 (Print)
Printed in the United States of America

Library of Congress Registration Number:
TXu 1-889-816, TXu 1-805-949 and TXu 2-092-284

To the ladies who sit up tall
at the bar
Wendy, Monica, Simone,
Melody, Suzie, Jeanie, Jackie, Jill,
Patti, Diane, and both Mary's

CONTENTS

Fair thoughts and happy hours attend on you.

William Shakespeare

PREFACE

Nobody liked Happy Hour as much as my mom and dad. Hardworking self-employed parents of five, they deserved a treat on the weekends, and we were taught to respect that. Only, their bar was at our home where our mother would mix her favorite "highball" and dad would have a "cold one" hidden in the back of the refrigerator.

My parents wrote music in their leisure time, like I write stories, and for the love of it. They inspired me to use my imagination to the utmost. And I do believe I do.

These stories require only one thing from you – allow yourself to slip into the shoes of my quirky characters and let them take you places you may have never gone before. Girlfriends, widows, innocent dupes, strangers, green-eyed monsters, ghostly spirits, they're all here on these pages waiting to entertain you, just like in the movies.

Along with some flash fiction, the poems you will run across are short, simple, and clear. Some of them are lyrics to songs I've written. None are too lofty or over your head – just playful little tidbits in rhyme.

I hope you will abandon yourself to pleasure while reading my fourth collection of stories, and please let me know if you do.

For the fun of it!

Libby Belle

HAPPY HOUR FOOLS

Happy hour
Friday afternoon
The sun is bright
Damn dark is this room

Wine half price
Oh, how nice
Calamari, bruschetta, mushrooms

At a black granite bar
A girl can go far
Sitting high on brown leather stools

Stay too long she'll start to belong
To the club of the happy hour fools

SPELLBOUND

*I*t's at Happy Hour when I meet my single girlfriends these days, Madelyn, Celeste, and Judy. I learned soon enough how easily men can sniff out a freshly divorced woman, so surrounding myself with "my girls" is like having a small fortress of protection. Protection from what, I'm not quite sure, but I do have a lot to learn about being single again, and for the time being, I'll just sit back and enjoy watching.

Our Happy Hours take place at Jacques, a finely designed restaurant bar separated from the main dining area by a half-wall accentuated with creamy translucent fabric. Lit to perfection it boasts a slick black twenty-foot-long slab of granite that accommodates our gluteus maximus quite comfortably on padded leather stools that swivel without squeaking. Underneath and within reach are those wonderful hooks for our big-ass designer purses that could easily carry a batch of new-born puppies or tote a change of clothing, including a pair of cowgirl boots. Behind the bar are three female bartenders all dressed in conservative black shirts and tight leggings. When they climb up on a step stool and reach high for a bottle of "the good stuff," only then can the men silently admire the shape of their tushes while the women attempt to read the tiny tattoos on their ankles.

One can also eat at the bar with access to a full menu, which tames the illusion that the patrons are there to get drunk or pick up a date for the night. Although this happens more than we like to admit, we pretend not to notice, lest we taint the bar's image.

Madelyn always arrives first. She likes to come early and set the scene with her ample breasts pouring out of a stretchy brightly patterned polyester blouse. Her fingernails are generally painted the color of ripened strawberries with matching toes squeezed into three-inch wedge heels. She has shiny black Barbie Doll hair, thin enough to twirl into a bun with ease, long enough to drape over her bare shoulders and into her lover's faces. With perfectly applied make-up, she looks like a woman who never washes the dishes, cleans a toilet, or vacuums out crumbs from her Mercedes convertible. But the truth is, she does all those things and more. She has a toolbox that most men would drool over, and because she has a heart of gold, she even built a doghouse for the neighbor's Rottweiler. No one would guess that she owns six pairs of stylish readers used for long corporate hours solving complex problems on pages and pages of charts that seem to never end. Her travels are not booked for elaborate excursions abroad or long lazy cruises, but primarily for business. In fact, this striking, single woman in her forties has never left the country. Not yet anyway.

If you look deep into Madelyn's hypnotic hazel eyes, you can see scars from years of pent-up anger living with a hopeless gambler who nearly broke her financially and emotionally. Until one day she woke up and sent him flying out the door, leaving her stuck with a stack of bills – which as the breadwinner she was already paying anyway while he lumped around pretending to be invisible, stealing from her savings account, her purse, and the loose change jar. She is intent on making up for all those fruitless years, and it's inspiring to watch her do so – one gorgeous man at a time.

When Celeste shows up, Madelyn dismisses the men who have gathered breathlessly around her and directs Celeste to the stool she saved for her. Knowing how hard it is to save a seat at this popular bar, Celeste is grateful and to show Madelyn how grateful, she ignores the flock of hopeful men and gives her a playful "faire la bise" on both cheeks. She'll acknowledge the hungry wolves only when Madelyn decides to make an introduction, and not until then. Respecting each other's territory has kept their friendship honest and their claws retracted.

Celeste has eyes that burst with energy and a wicked smile that makes men move in closer. She is Scandinavian and having spent her life equally between Northern Europe and Texas, she has this wonderful little crunchy sound in her warm and inviting voice. She wears her red-streaked hair in a Pixie cut with a sexy long bang that frames one side of her face and swoops below her chin, revealing a wide flawless forehead that tells you how intelligent and fearless she can be. She's funny, too and laughs at her own jokes long before she's finished telling them, which puts everyone listening in a lighthearted mood. But behind that sanguine personality is an emotionally fraught tender-hearted woman burdened with a troubled past she is determined to bury.

Celeste is also the youngest of our group. She's in her late thirties and looks like she's fresh out of her twenties. She's unapologetically candid and confesses that her fountain of youth is Botox. Being in the medical field, she can offer a generous discount to her friends. I choose not to participate, explaining that the wrinkles I've earned are so deeply embedded, there's not enough botulism bacteria in the world to smooth out these ruts.

Judy is one of the bartenders who we have adopted, and she's older than all of us, but full of vim and vigor with a rump shaped like a cantaloupe and a glowing skin tone like caramelized sugar. Below gold-rimmed eyeglasses are a set of naturally contoured cheekbones that she proudly claims were inherited from her Bolivian father, while the full blood-red lips were a gift from her African mother. She cunningly eased her way into our lives by telling us that she has heard all our conversations from behind the bar and knows us intimately. Armed with all that personal information, we decided she had to be brought into the group, so she was officially initiated over a round of shots. A good move on our part, because now she gives us the lowdown on the patrons in exchange for padding her tips. We don't see Judy out in the real world. Her struggles are far beyond our help, but we love and respect her and appreciate the double shifts she takes to make life better for her family.

We ladies don't talk on the phone or email the latest news. We hold it all in until we meet at the bar and spill our guts, but never our drinks.

Madelyn is crazy about a wealthy man heading toward a lengthy and dreadful divorce. This infatuation has hung on for two years too long with no sign of the "Big D" on the court dockets yet. It seems the wife has suddenly decided she prefers women instead of men and is getting much more satisfaction out of torturing and embarrassing him. No one can predict how long they can play this awful game and how long Madelyn will wait. But she's today's modern woman and will not let that stop her from enjoying the fine men that fall into her lap. Still, I see the hurt in her eyes when she talks about him. She's under a spell I would cast on no one I care about.

Celeste is in love with her freedom, her new body, and her personal trainer – a perfect man with a rippling six-pack. Unfortunately, he died from a sudden heart attack before he could declare his love for her. Both were too stubborn to reveal their true feelings for one another, and now it is too late. I can see the hurt in her eyes when she doesn't talk about him. She is still under his spell even though he's no longer around to spot her at the gym.

Judy, Judy, Judy. She's the gal that everybody wants to hug. With a mischievous twinkle in her eye, her breathy soft-spoken drawl can talk a bank robber into confessing where he hid the dough. She has an uncanny way of guessing what you're thinking before you even think it. Unlike the rest of us, she found her man early on and married at twenty. They divorced and remarried twice over twenty-five years of crazy love. Seems they're both under some kind of ongoing spell and can't live apart for too long. Currently they're split up, and she hates him with a passion, but she is achingly waiting for that magical day when they will get back together and start the cycle all over again. Her spell is worse than any I've ever seen, and it wears me out trying to understand it.

Observing my friends bewitched like this, I can assure you I will never let that happen to me.

By the time I arrive, my girls have slipped into a comfort zone that will take me a little longer to register. I don't always come to the bar just to relax or chat with them. Because I'm in marketing, I like eavesdropping on the conversations surrounding me and exchanging ideas with strangers – engaging them in subjects that don't include the weather. A great deal of information can be gathered from places like this. It is amazing what others will share, especially after a few drinks, and the conversations vary depending on the beverage they're enjoying.

For instance, I have noticed that martini sipping women tend to brag a lot and talk about their latest purchases. With crossed legs, they seductively slip their fingers in and out of thin straps on shiny new high heels while skillfully balancing a wide-mouthed cocktail glass. They usually demand lots of space.

The beer drinkers, slouched and relaxed, act as if they are at home in front of a football game and sports is their main topic. They never once try to squeeze in their gut, and inevitably, one out of three wears a baseball cap.

The cold refreshing blend of spirits and exotic flavors in the hands of the cocktail lovers goes down as quickly as their fast and fierce opinions. Sometimes you can feel their sting all the way down at the end of the bar.

The "liquor is quicker" patrons are emboldened by the "neat" drink that marches straight to their brains, and with little effort, they can throw you under the bus talking politics or tell a story that will curl your toes. I would avoid eating while in their grasp.

The wine drinkers, oh yes, there are plenty of them. They ponder life, the meaning of everything, and before they know it, they are hunkered down with the person seated next to them sharing their appetizers in deep conversation, as everyone else in the room slowly disappears.

I confess that on occasion, wine makes even me hunker. And now is probably the right time to describe me. I've been told I'm easy on the eye but not easily read; a mystery underneath my jeans and conservative rolled-up-sleeve cotton shirts. My hair is wavy, and a good ole honest brown with limited streaks of blonde and probably too short for my extra tall frame. How tall am I? Well, I was the girl in school who was placed with the boys on the top row of the bleachers in all our group pictures. Tall enough! It's been implied that I should wear more make-up, and once a nose-job was recommended. But to put it simply, a kind man once told me, 'I see *you* first, before I see you.' It was meant to be flattering, but if I think about it too long, I'm not quite sure.

The truth is, men rarely look my way because their eyes are mainly on the sea of younger cleavages lined up at the bar. Oblivious to their own gaping mouths, they stare like my sons did when they were little watching me apply lipstick. That dumbfounded look of awe is precious on boys, but not so cute when seen on grown men with jowls and whiskers. I can't help but laugh inwardly, and sometimes it's painful to watch them suffering like that. As we southern women often say with ease, "Bless their little hearts."

There are some men we like more than others, and when they are all there at once, they're easy game. Celeste gets their attention with her latest enhancement. She is so proud, she jerked me into the restroom, lifted her blouse and proclaimed with those huge green eyes, "See my new boobs!" as if she were showing me a new purse. I've never seen her so excited, so I had to adjust my attitude about cosmetic surgery. And the truth is, they did look perky.

I'm a naturalist and my breasts are what they are. They've provided nourishment for two children and pleasure for a husband that at one time told me they could fill a champagne coupé glass perfectly. He ruined it by further telling me that Marie Antoinette designed the glass with a mold from her left breast. So, for years my breasts were named Marie and Antoinette. I suppose that could be one of the few highlights from my divorce – that beheaded Queen of France is no longer living in my bra.

In this collection of fine men, there is one whom I'm secretly attracted to. His name is Logan. In fact, he's the only Logan I've ever met. I haven't felt this kind of tug in a long time, and although we casually chat, I remain elusive. I'm somewhat unnerved by this man who reminds me so much of my ex-husband, sometimes I can barely take my eyes off him. His striking appearance is turning every woman's head within thirty feet. My ex-husband had the same effect on women. It ended up being his downfall. Another story with a sad ending I wish I could rewrite, or at least edit.

Oddly enough, Madelyn pulls back and doesn't give Logan the time of day, and unless you know her like I do, this is out of character. She has a wonderfully healthy libido and excels in casual flirtations. She explains to me later that he's the kind who is attracted only to younger women. She won't waste her time. Celeste, however, easily grabs his attention. Although she claims she is simply brushing up on her flirting and that he is much too old for her, I think it bothers Madelyn to see Logan's playful connection with Celeste. Beautiful Madelyn is not used to being ignored. Even if she wants to be.

One night I went to the bar hoping no one I knew was there. I felt especially lonely and not interested in small talk or listening to the same stories. Even Judy must have sensed my dark mood and kept her distance, allowing another bartender to take my order. I sat quietly by myself, toying with the absurd idea of calling my ex-husband while mindlessly poking at a spinach salad, until you know who sits right next to me. Logan, with his cute, crooked smile and sad bedroom eyes. His long torso and wide shoulders sit neatly next to mine; a familiarity I have missed. We seem to be in a similar nostalgic mood, and without others around to interrupt, we talk as if we've known each other forever. Our carefree conversation easily opens our hearts. He is a widower of four years, and tears still well up when he talks about her. Sharing pictures of his saintly wife and their perfect children, he tells me in a soft voice of her terrible ending. Head-to-head, I briefly share the death of my marriage. And now, I am sadder than ever and undeniably enamored with a man six years younger than me who enjoys many women of his choosing, yet keeps his heart buried with his wife.

We close down the bar followed by a warm hug and agreeing that we had a lovely conversation. I watch him fade away into the dark parking lot. His beautiful broad back is the last thing I see, and the first thing I see when I shut my eyes later that evening. While drifting off to sleep, I hear an alert from my cell phone. It's a text message from Logan. 'Let's find time to talk again. You ground me.' A start of a new friendship? I respond too quickly with a resounding *Yes!* Too late to delete the exclamation mark. I'm just glad I used only one.

The next few times I see Logan at the bar, he's with his tennis buddies. He is polite, acknowledges me with a simple nod and goes about tending to them. Our last meeting is now long forgotten, lost in an alcohol haze. I am careful not to look his way, but naturally, we catch each other's eye and exchange smiles, and that is as far as it goes. I am relieved that I'm smart enough not to expect more.

I arrived early one night at Jacques ahead of the girls, and not by choice I'm sitting at the bar with Tiff, a woman who I haven't seen in months. My girls despise her. She is a kind of vixen sexy in a clingy dress, laced at the scoop of the neck, outlining her cleavage with a daintiness that doesn't suit her burnt tan and orange flipflops. She has just finished telling me why she hasn't frequented the bar lately. It seems she was being stalked by her last married lover and had to lay low. Confident that he's no longer lurking, she shifts into position and goes on the prowl, scanning the room for the next lucky dupe. Anxiously, she shares another story with me about having sex with her dermatologist, right in his office during an official visit. "It just happened," she laughingly explains and adds boastfully, "I had to go back for several mole removals since then."

I am aghast and thought I had heard it all until now, and I'm wishing my girls were here to take some of the pressure off my ears. Instead, Logan shows up, and sits on the only stool left at the bar next to Tiff, the sex kitten whose eyes perk up right along with her lacy breasts when I introduce them. Within minutes, no, make that seconds, Tiff stashes her wad of gum under the bar and makes a ninety degree swivel his direction. Now, all I see is her freckled boney shoulder blades while they are chatting and laughing as I slowly, achingly evaporate.

Later, in the ladies' room, Tiff tells me from the adjacent stall that she really likes Logan and has a date already lined up. I respond dully through the shared wall, "Yes, he is likable," and I drown out my disappointment with the loud reverberating flush of the toilet – twice!

Bypassing them at the bar, I escape unnoticed into the restless night air to sit with the smokers out on the deck. I look around me at the satisfaction on their faces as their brain releases adrenaline for that quick buzz of pleasure. I feel like I'm back in college, and for the first time ever, I wish I liked cigarettes.

To hell with it! I bummed one off the elderly lady smoking Virginia Slims and lit up.

As I sit there wondering if I'll smell like cigarette smoke later, I ask myself, "Can it be that I am under Logan's spell? Impossible! Inconceivable! No way!"

But I cannot lie to the person I trust the most…me. I am spellbound! Oh, good lord, how embarrassing! At my age?"

I stayed away from my favorite bar the next few weeks to shake off this bizarre feeling I certainly will not share with the girls.

There are other nice places I can go to other than Jacques, and this time my good friend, Trent has joined me, and we are having a nice chat over lasagna. A guitar player is singing lovesick melodies barely heard over the voices from the talkative crowd of millennials who have taken over the place. The music makes me melancholy, and I share with Trent how odd I've been feeling lately and how I've conjured up all these old feelings for my ex-husband, mainly because of a man I met at the bar, leaving out his name, of course. And wouldn't you know it, just when he reaches over to console me, Logan and Tiff appear before us. *Oh my god, he's still seeing her!* There's no room at the bar, Tiff claims, eyeing the two empty chairs at our table. Through glazed eyes, I introduce them, and of course, I invite them to sit. It seems I am a glutton for punishment.

We order more drinks and talk about things that don't matter. The light is brighter in the dining area, and I feel oddly exposed. Trying desperately to avoid Logan's eyes, I guess it's so obvious, even mindless Tiff senses my unusual discomfort. When Logan excuses himself to the men's room, she slinks into the seat next to me and whispers in my ear, "I really like him. Thanks for introducing us."

"Of course. I'm glad you like each other," I answer with a bold-faced lie and am not happy with myself for that. Normally, as a matchmaker at heart, I would be pleased to have introduced people who end up dating. But even the muse in me is hoping that Tiff is not planning on torturing me with more talk of Logan, and to make sure she doesn't, I lasso Trent into the conversation, and he expertly changes the subject.

Logan returns, we order another round, and I invite the musician over to the table for a diversion that I badly need. I casually immerse myself into enjoying the men, leaving Logan in the skillful hands of the black widow.

Later, I chastise myself for having these childish adolescent feelings of envy and an underlying disappointment in Logan for choosing the floozy over smart and elegant Madelyn. I know better than to allow myself any cockeyed delusions that I could ever be considered one of his possibilities. To help me move past this ridiculous infliction, I call up a man I like to see on occasion and invite him out for drinks. I'm missing Jacques, Judy, the staff, and the regulars, so we plan to meet there.

It's a full moon outside, and as predicted, my girls show up and my date's head swells with all the attention they give him. I'm perfectly fine with that. They are darling, younger, vibrant women who dress for men, and that fully illuminated moon is no doubt energizing their sexual desires. Plus, he deserves their consideration because he knows I will not take him to my bed. Why? I'm really not sure, except, I'm not ready yet, or I'm being silly, or I'm under this stupid spell.

But I am relaxed and easygoing until Logan shows up, Tiff sniffing at his heels like a nervous wiener dog. Judy gives me a sour face that makes me chuckle but also brings me to my senses, because even though I feel disgust looking at them together, I need to get used to this. But how? I look over at my posse who are watching the whole scene and catch the disappointment in Madelyn's eyes, and the look of disdain on Celeste's face, and now I am burdened with the task of making my girls feel better, too.

My date had to leave early, so there goes that buffer. I

can't stop myself from glancing over at Logan, who is looking at me, a look on his face I've never seen before. Was that a cry for help? Don't kid yourself. But in that split second when our eyes take hold, I have the strangest, almost spiritual out of body experience: The room is suddenly frozen in a perfect bubble of stillness, a quiet I haven't experienced since I floated over the ocean in a hot-air balloon. Right before my eyes I see me and Logan as two ghostly spirits hand in hand gliding through the lifeless people in a graceful waltz. There is a peace like no other in our blissful wake. Is that "Beauty and the Beast" I hear?

As we reach the exit, he turns to kiss me. My eyes flutter when feeling his warm breath caressing my cheek. *Barely even friends, then somebody bends, unexpectedly...*

And just before our lips meet, the bubble bursts!

Jolted out of the mystical trance, I open my eyes and hear the patrons all around me talking louder than ever, as if someone had turned up the volume. Logan shrugs at my obviously weird expression and turns his attention to Tiff who is pressing her body hard against his.

Startlingly aware of the awkward scene and my foolish infatuation with this man, I feel like an idiot and quickly move through the crowd toward my girls.

We huddle at the end of the bar.

Judy slides into the conversation, pretends to be taking our order and leans in closer, not wanting to miss a single word.

"She's not all *that* cute," Celeste lightly snorts, takes a swig of her drink and dramatically throws her head back in annoyance.

"I could care less about the man," Madelyn spouts, sucking in her cheeks. "I have promised my guy that I'll be monogamous from now on. He thinks the divorce is getting closer."

"You know," Judy's scratchy voice is barely heard from behind the bar, "her days are numbered. He'll have another just like her in a week or two. I've seen it before with him. Just watch. Poor guy can't get past his dead wife."

Our heads turn simultaneously to look at the best catch in the room, and there is a collective sigh by all.

"But what about that look Logan gave *you?*" Celeste cunningly asks me.

"Yes, and the look we saw you give him back," Madelyn prods, her curious eyes and Judy's searching mine. "Your eyes even closed. What's happening here?"

I turned away from the three nymphs waiting impatiently for some sort of explanation. I don't need to explain myself. Why should I? They could not possibly understand what transpired between me and Logan the night we sat alone at the bar sharing our worlds. Like magic, he became the husband I lost, and I became his deceased wife, and in that one fleeting moment, as if our deepest sorrows had vanished, there was a spark of pure happiness between two broken hearts that will never be together.

Just then, Tiff flip flops past us on her way to the restroom. The girls roll their eyes as she passes.

I head the opposite direction. "Where are you going?" Madelyn yells from behind me.

I tell all three of them with a wink and a devilish smile, "I need to take care of some unfinished business." I sense their confused eyes plastered on me as I walk away.

Now, there comes a time in a woman's life when she must buck up and break her own spell. Waiting for someone or something to do it for her is downright irresponsible. I knew what I needed to do, and the timing was too perfect. Energized, with my head held high, I walked purposely up to Logan and tapped him on the shoulder. He turned around and smiled. "What's up?" he asked with wet blameless eyes.

Not wasting a precious second of my newfound courage, I stepped up high on my toes, wrapped my arms around his neck and planted a light, but long loving kiss on his luscious full lips. He instinctively, however timidly, kissed me back. I allowed the kiss to last long enough to burn it in my memory. Such a prince, he let me pull away first. When I did, his eyes appeared as round as saucers and his cheeks as red as cherry tomatoes. I can't help but smile at his honest reaction.

"I just wanted to thank you for the waltz," I said, ever so sincerely, because I had come to realize that Logan, although innocently, had given me the gift of hope for the love still alive inside me. But before I say more and mess up a most exquisite moment, I twirl around in what feels like slow motion, give a little wave to my obviously stunned girls, and without looking back, I walk weightlessly out of the restaurant into an enchanting moonlit night.

And that, ladies, is how you break a spell.

MAPLE SYRUP KISS

*E*leanor's husband of sixteen years died so quickly, it took a month for everyone to accept that he was actually dead and not hiding out somewhere damp and dark working nonstop on one of his crazy inventions. A short, cute, and clever man hit the wall running, and everyone who knew him was truly heartbroken. Will, with his sexy smile, was the kind of man women adored, and his generosity went way beyond the norm, always lending a hand, money, his lawnmower, and his strong back to anyone in need. His jokes – corny, dirty, ridiculous – kept everyone entertained. Will's inimitable facial expressions, his infectious laughter, along with a substantial nose that could sniff out a liar in seconds flat, could send the entire room into rounds of unfettered hilarity.

Yes, it was a sad day when they lost Will and his beautiful inventive mind.

Since his death, Eleanor had very few visitors. She was told more than once by Will's spiteful sister that she had been lucky enough to live in his shadow. Now, there was no shadow, and it had been so long since Eleanor had seen her own, she worried if she'd ever find it again.

Before Will, she had traveled the world playing for various symphony orchestras. Men came and left, some lovers, some friends, but they always had a warm hug for her should they casually meet again. Eleanor left no man angry, bitter, or sad. She was married to her cello, and they respected that, or at least, accepted that. An only child, both parents deceased, she went through life purely, without fantasies or expectations, compact and sensible, until she met William Franklin White.

To this day she cannot explain what magical force came over her when they first met at the airport: There he stood, leaning against the wall, reading a magazine, his feet crossed at the ankles, an old tattered leather bag looped over his shoulder, the sleeves of his white shirt unevenly rolled up, a tie loosened below three unfastened buttons, and that thick unruly pre-mature silvery hair shooting all different directions, naturally parted on the side, a long wavy bang dangling over one eye. She dragged her small piece of luggage to the only unoccupied chair just inches from his knees and sat down. She looked up at him, and he looked down at her, his smile broad and clean, twinkling eyes beneath Santa Claus eyebrows, dimples so deep, she thought the tip of her finger could get lost in them.

"Oh, this isn't your seat, is it?" she asked, suddenly aware that she may have just stolen it.

"If it is, it's yours now," he smiled wider, his green eyes flashing, a warning sign if Eleanor ever saw one.

"I'm sorry. I just assumed...." She got up to relinquish the only available chair in the waiting area.

"Just kidding," Will said, gently taking her arm and leading her back to the seat.

Eleanor felt the heat from his hand radiate through her thin blouse. She tentatively thanked him and quickly removed a letter from her purse and began reading it, leaving the attractive man to his magazine. While she read, she couldn't help but look at his shoes, black high tops with the casual slacks stuffed inside them, his jacket rumpled up on the floor. He was standing so close, she surreptitiously let her eyes trail his body, stopping at his groin where the fabric had tented. She looked elsewhere, trying to bite away a smile.

"Don't move," Will whispered in her ear. "There's something in your hair. Let me get it out."

"What?" Eleanor raised her hand to feel the top of her head.

Will grabbed it and gently led it back to her lap. "You don't want to touch this, I promise."

She felt him ruffle her hair, as she hunched over in fearful anticipation of what he was removing.

"Got it!" he claimed. "Keep an eye on my things, please. This needs to be disposed of and now!"

Eleanor watched him reach the trash can and throw something into it, a look of disgust on his face. She was horrified.

When he came back to the wall, that cocky smile returning, she looked up at him, her mouth twisted, almost afraid to ask, "What was it?"

"You don't want to know," he shook his head and raised his eyebrows, his lips tightened, as if to warn her not to ask again.

"Of course, I want to know. Good heavens, what was in my hair? Maybe there's more!"

"I don't think there's anymore, but if I tell you, it'll bug you the rest of the day."

Eleanor cautiously tapped her fingers on her scalp and just as she did, boarding instructions were announced. Will bowed before her and clicked his heels, "Nice to meet you...*and* your friend," he laughed, walking determinedly away to get in line.

"Well, of all the nerve!" Eleanor huffed, gathering up her things, steering her body away from the trash can and filing in line with the other passengers. She stood watching the back of Will's head, shiny locks of hair curling up at the ends just below his collar. His back was broad, and his rear-end was high and tight, one leg of his pants tucked in the high-top, the other nearly touching the floor. Even though charming was written all over this man, his posture said *rebel*. Still, she was not about to spend the rest of the flight not knowing what was in her hair. She would be sure to ask him again if she got the chance. And surprisingly, she found herself wishing for that chance.

Will chose a seat next to the window and whenever someone would start to claim the seat next to him, he'd tell them that he was saving it for his friend. When Eleanor came down the aisle, he jumped up and politely picked up her bag and put it in the overhead bin. Then he casually pointed to the seat he had saved. Eleanor sat down pretending to be perturbed, leaving the smiles for later.

They ended up talking and laughing during the entire flight, although Will refused to tell her what had been in her hair. He promised he'd share at dinner the following night. Eleanor canceled the date she had with another cello player, a date that would not have ended up in her hotel room, and from then on, she was without question, under Will's spell.

Will had been married once before, and Eleanor, single in her late thirties with no delusions of grandeur, required only a modest wedding in a small church, surrounded by a handful of friends. From there they continued to lead a scheduled life with both often traveling different directions. Eventually they moved into a small cottage by a river in the graceful hills of Connecticut where Will had spent his childhood and sold his first invention.

All those years together and Will never did tell Eleanor what was in her hair that day in the airport. "He's so stubborn, I'll have to wait until he's on his deathbed to get it out of him," she'd say. And that's exactly when he finally told her.

She sat quietly at the foot of his bed, watching the nurses come and go, adjusting the pain medicine, fluffing his pillow, waiting for his smile to make their day. Even though his life was hanging on by a thread, he never failed to give them the *Cool Hand Luke* smile that made them totally forget his wife was in the room and still made Eleanor weak in the knees.

"You'd like to know, wouldn't you?" he reached out for her hand.

Eleanor put her hand in his. Will had a habit of rubbing the callouses on the tips of her fingertips. She knew he was too weak to do something even as simple as that, and at that moment she felt a deep sadness knowing how much she would miss those small affectionate gestures.

"Like to know what?" she asked.

"What was in your hair when we first met," he said so softly, she could barely hear him.

She playfully squeezed his hand. "Oh, so *now* you're going to tell me."

"There was nothing in your hair, my dear. Nothing."

"Nothing? But I saw you throw it away." Eleanor stood over him, looking down into his glazed eyes.

A sudden sparkle appeared when he said, "There was

nothing. I just wanted to get your attention. And I did, didn't I?"

"Oh, Will. All these years and it was nothing? You stinker!"

"Yes, I am, aren't I?"

On that same day, with his last ounce of energy, Will gave Eleanor a final loving smile before closing his eyes on the girl of his dreams.

There were times during that first year of grieving, Eleanor sat quietly with her cello and tried desperately to recall the days before Will, when she had been so fiercely independent. He had spoiled her, protected her, and became her voice. She rarely had to think at all and was completely unprepared for the impending battle over the will, instigated by his angry, militant sister who had the audacity to blame Eleanor for her brother's death.

His closest friends offered little support; coming and going, staying just long enough to remind her that she was on her own. Intermittent phone calls filled with words of wisdom from her friends who lived all over the country were forgotten the minute she hung up. Weary from it all, she sold the house and moved into a small condo near the airport. She placed herself back in the music scene and took assignments to play in national orchestras.

It was time to find her lost shadow.

Another year rolled by when Eleanor finally accepted her first date since the death of her husband. The man was a local rancher with the hearty nickname, Grizz, short for Griswold. Tall, ruggedly handsome, and a widower, she had met him at a restaurant while outside listening to a string quartet, sitting under a canopy sparsely scattered with classical music lovers. He pulled a chair up beside her and offered to buy her a drink. The sweet setting, the misty rain, and the ancient music kept their conversation simple and innocent, and a date was easily arranged.

A half dozen more dates with Grizz followed. Eleanor had yet to draw any conclusions about the man until she caught him tossing his wife's ashes into the botanical gardens where they were visiting. Shaken, but somehow relieved, he confessed that every place he had taken Eleanor was also where he had taken his wife while she was alive. He went on to confess that on each of their dates he had secretly sprinkled an ounce of his wife's ashes in gardens or flowerpots in commemoration of their outings together. Eleanor needed some time to digest what he had shared before she would respond, but it did explain why he never gave her a goodnight kiss at the end of their dates. The poor man was still grieving, and she of all people knew what that meant.

Dinner was planned at Grizz's home and Eleanor was a bit apprehensive about seeing his place for the first time. When she entered the house, she knew why. Pictures of his deceased wife were placed on every wall, on every tabletop, and even in the kitchen on the refrigerator. When Grizz took her to his bedroom and walked her inside his wife's closet, this is when Eleanor decided the relationship must end. He ran his hands dreamily through the hundreds of dresses, blouses, skirts, and scarves. He admiringly pointed out fifty-two boxes of shoes, and when he caressed a gold slipper in his hand as if it were a newborn kitten and sat it down next to his own shoe, Eleanor pictured him trying to slip it on his size twelve foot. The funny scene made her stifle an inappropriate laugh that temporarily masked the uneasiness growing inside her. Looking her up and down he surmised, "You're about her size, you know." Then he selected a polka-dotted dress and held it against her body, as if he were a saleslady in a dress store. "This is one of my favorites. I would love to see it on you. My wife spared no expense and some of these outfits cost well over a hundred dollars each."

Eleanor hid in the bathroom as long as possible and waited until Grizz announced that the steaks were grilled to perfection. She packaged one up in aluminum foil, split the salad she had brought in half, and on her way out the door, she gave her regards to the lifelike picture of the deceased wife hanging in the entry. Without a word, she kissed Grizz on the forehead and left him standing on the porch scratching his dog's head in confusion; the entire chocolate cake she had baked sat untouched on his wife's kitchen table.

Following that fiasco, she dated off and on, and it seemed as if she was getting all the leftovers from the dating scene. There was Adam, a cute sturdy cowboy in lizard boots with jeans so tight, she seriously wondered where his testicles had gone. She found out none too soon that they were in the hands of his wife.

Next was Farley, freshly divorced and couldn't remember how to date, and after reading so many magazines about the new emerging super woman he was even afraid to open the door for one. Eleanor was not in the mood to teach him.

She even went as far as dating twin brothers, Ted and Ed, and not able to tell them apart – their little game was not to reveal their true identity – she strongly announced to Ted, or was it, Ed, "Whoever you are, both of you, please don't call me again."

Flip was probably the nicest man she had gone out with and the one with potential, but he had a girlfriend on the side who Eleanor found out about when she picked up a phone call while waiting at his apartment one day. They talked for the longest, both finally agreeing to give him up, and to meet later that week for drinks. Come to find out, Louise was a jewel, and just the kind of friend Eleanor needed. A no-nonsense woman like herself who admitted that she could live without men but would rather not. They spent the next year solving the world's problems over dinners, at the gym, and on weekend excursions to places where they were told men were abundant.

It was in her third year of winters when Louise took a brave step forward and moved to South Carolina. "You should come too, Eleanor. These winters are killing me, and I'm tired of hiding out from my ex-husband."

Eleanor wanted to leave. She had always wanted to leave, but Connecticut was where Will was buried. This was where he was happiest. She needed a sign.

Praying fervently one afternoon, she cried herself to sleep sprawled out on the living room floor after a round of muscle stretches. She had a dream that she was cooking a pot of soup on the stove, and as she did, her apron caught on fire from the high flame. She saw herself running around the room trying to put it out, her yells for help stifled as if sealed inside a jar. Forced awake by the fire alarm piercing her ears, she bolted to the kitchen in a panic. Nothing was on the stove, but coming from underneath the pantry door, she saw smoke. She instinctively grabbed her purse and ran outside. Billows of heavy smoke poured from the condo next door. Her neighbor had gotten out with nothing but her shoes and was standing there helplessly watching her world go up in flames.

"My cello!" Eleanor cried in a sudden realization.

Back inside, the smoke was filling the kitchen and on its way down the hall to her bedroom. Eleanor drug a box full of photos and music from the hall closet, grabbed the cello and managed to snatch a picture of Will standing in front of one of his inventions, getting them out just as the first flame licked at the pantry door.

Eleanor thought to run to each condo and warn the residents. People were already filing out of their homes, dragging their personal belongings to their cars. An elderly man struggled with his rocking chair, an heirloom from his mother. Eleanor spent the next hour helping all those she could until finally, the fire department drowned out the angry flames that had consumed five of the twenty-two units, including hers.

Well, she had asked for a sign, and she damn well got one! *Things are just things.* She counted her blessings, so few since Will died. In tears, she called Louise and by the end of the week, she was on her way to South Carolina with her cello taking up the whole back seat and still in search of her shadow.

Louise had a lovely home, an extra bedroom, and a wonderful attitude. She had never been happier and greeted Eleanor with joy in her heart. It would take time to get the insurance settlement, and time to adjust, and Louise put no restraints on her friend and made the transition easy.

One evening, Louise came home flushed with excitement. She had met a man, a darling man with good teeth and a great sense of humor. "And to top it off, he has a head full of hair!" After two dates, she invited him to dinner, and asked Eleanor to join them. He would bring along a friend to make the evening a foursome. Of course, there would be no expectations on Eleanor's part, and she could relax knowing that more than anything Louise wanted her there to sum up this new man in her life; someone she just might be able to sink her teeth in.

Eleanor dressed down, wanting Louise to be the highlight of the evening. She helped her pick out the perfect dress to enhance her lovely auburn hair. Excitement and apple pie from the oven filled the air as they cooked a wonderful meal together, pairing it with the best wine. Candles were lit, and both agreed that Tony Bennet's album would be a good start, followed by The Zombies, a favorite from their era, ending with Simon and Garfunkel.

Ready for the evening, Eleanor sat on the sofa sipping a glass of wine, while Louise brushed her teeth for the third time that day and added another layer of hair spray to her curls. The doorbell rang, and Louise popped her head out from the bedroom, "Get that please, and tell Ray I need another minute. Hope the other guy is cute," she winked.

Eleanor opened the door, the wine glass still in her hand. She greeted the men and stepped aside to let them enter. She didn't know either of them, but the shorter man looked so much like her deceased husband, she nearly dropped her drink. Before they could introduce themselves, Louise entered the room. Eleanor had never seen her like this, holding the edge of her full skirt in one hand, the other twirling a scarf in the air as if she were about to perform. Giddy! She was simply giddy. Her flirtatious smile directed at the shorter man quickly dropped when she saw the man standing behind him.

"Umm," the shorter man tore his gaze from Louise and cleared his throat, "I'm Ray." He held his hand out to Eleanor, "And this is Dirk." Eleanor shook their hands and looked back at Louise who had not moved a muscle, still standing there looking dumbfounded, still holding the scarf in the air. An awkward moment for all.

"Hi Louise," Dirk said, sheepishly shrugging his shoulders, an innocent Charlie Brown smile spread crookedly across his face.

Eleanor looked from Dirk to Louise, "Do you two know each other?"

"Well, you could say that. I was married to our guest for nearly twenty years," she claimed, finally allowing herself to smile.

Ray slapped his knee and laughed. "If this doesn't take the cake! Look what the cat dragged in! Your ex-husband!"

Eleanor covered her mouth and laughed with him, timorously glancing over at Louise for a sign. Was the laughing acceptable, or should the ex-husband be kicked out the door? But when Dirk let go of his muffled laugh, Louise couldn't resist and joined in the fun.

Drinks were passed around and as everyone began to relax, Louise pried the details from Ray about how he knew her ex-husband. With it all out on the table, they moved on to dinner. Eleanor said nothing about how much Ray reminded her of Will, and she managed to hold back her delight.

As they dined, the conversation easily split up between the four, and at one point, Louise fell into casual talk with Dirk, while Ray told Eleanor a few of his favorite jokes. Not only did he look like Will, perhaps not as handsome, he had a similar demeanor and a sharp wit to match. Before the night was over, the four of them were comfortably numb from the alcohol and enjoying the topics of the evening over hot apple pie.

When it was time for the gentlemen to leave, Louise walked Ray outside, as the men had come in separate cars. Dirk stayed dutifully behind and chatted with Eleanor.

"Looks like they hit it off," he said with a wink from across the room.

"It does. It's been a wonderful but unusual evening." Eleanor picked up the empty drink glasses and carried them to the kitchen. Dirk followed.

"I'm so sorry about your place burning down. How awful for you," he said with an earnestness Eleanor appreciated.

"Yes, it was. But I doubt I would've ever made it back down south if it hadn't. Truth is, I prayed for a sign right before it happened," she chuckled. "I didn't expect it to be such an obvious one. I'm kind of hardheaded."

"Signs, yeah, they're interesting. I'm trying to figure out if this is a sign. Me coming here tonight. Who would've thunk it?"

"You two have been divorced about five years now, is that right?" Eleanor asked, passing him a towel to dry the wine glasses.

"About. I haven't seen and have barely talked to Louise since, and I had no idea she moved back here until tonight. This was quite a shock…a pleasant one, mind you. We didn't leave each other on bad terms. We just…"

"Oh, so you stayed behind to help clean up, eh?" Louise interrupted the conversation. The lipstick smear was just enough to show that a kiss had taken place; her walk slightly off.

"I did." Dirk waved the towel to show off his domestic skill and flashed a boastful grin. "I didn't say this earlier… think it took a while to get over the coincidence, but I'm glad to see you. You look wonderful, Louise."

"Why, thank you," Louise sighed, kicking off her shoes. "You look pretty healthy yourself."

Eleanor closed the dishwasher and when she excused

herself for the evening, with neither of them objecting, she was sure it was the perfect time for an exit. "It was a pleasure meeting you, Dirk. I hope we get to see you and Ray again. Tonight, was nice. Goodnight, all."

The next morning at breakfast, the ladies had a good laugh over their dinner date. "Well, what'd you think? Ray's a cutie, isn't he?" Louise said, pouring herself a cup of coffee, while Eleanor popped bagels in the toaster.

"I'd say so. Very nice guy. And Dirk is, well, I'm not sure what to say. Do you want me to hate him, like him, or have him shot?"

Louise laughed, "We're not in high school anymore, honey. He's a likable guy. That never was our problem. What did you *really* think about him? I mean, would *you* date him?"

Eleanor wanted to tell her friend that Ray was more her style, but she wasn't about to put that in her head. Early-sixties or not, women still had jealous streaks, just not nearly as volatile without the hot flashes. "Well, first of all, he didn't ask me out, and secondly, that would depend on you. I mean, he was your man for a long time. How did you feel about seeing him again?"

Louise had to take a few seconds to think about that answer. "Honestly, I was a bit freaked out at first, but as the night went on, it felt good to be around him. Only…I really like Ray. Isn't he charming?"

"Very!" Eleanor responded much too emphatically and attempting to amend the remark, she added, "I mean, I can see why you are attracted to him. Think you'll see him again soon?"

"I do. We talked about having another dinner party at

his place this time. He thinks we all hit it off nicely last night, so if you're game, he wants us to come to dinner this Friday. Dirk said he'd love to see us again."

"I don't know why not." Eleanor rose from her chair. "But I'm out the door now. I have an appointment to view those new cottages going up on the East side. Might be an ideal next home for me. See you later."

Louise yelled from the kitchen, "You know, there's no rush in you moving out!"

"I know," Eleanor stuck her head back in the kitchen. "But if things get hot for you and Ray, well, you know what I'm saying," she winked and flashed a grin.

"We'll see," Louise said. "No rush for that either, but we'll see. He *is* a cutie." She lifted her cup in the air to toast to the idea. "And so is Dirk." She was glad Eleanor had not heard her deep sigh.

The second dinner together went well, and the following day the four of them met at the country club for brunch. Louise quickly positioned herself at the table next to Dirk, while Eleanor was left to sit next to Ray. She smiled awkwardly and gave an innocent shrug at the sudden move. They ordered the buffet and lined up to peruse the long table of delicacies, including fresh Mimosas, Eleanor's favorite. Louise pinched Dirk's shirt and pulled him toward the server making waffles. "Still love waffles?" she asked, playfully.

"I loved yours." He gave her a dopey smile. "Still make them like you used to?"

"Not as often as I'd like. No fun eating them without hearing your oohs and ahhs and watching you pour half a bottle of syrup on them."

The entire morning went by with Dirk and Louise carrying on about the things they remembered while married. Ray acted as if it was normal and told his usual jokes. Eleanor tried not to show how much she enjoyed him, and at one point she was so engrossed in Ray, she dabbed a glop of syrup from his face with a napkin in such a natural way, one would have thought they were a couple. A sudden memory of Will and the taste of maple syrup on his lips when they kissed while eating waffles in bed flashed before her. Unknowingly, she leaned in closer to Ray's face.

Louise gave her a funny look. Eleanor straightened up and stammered through an explanation, "Oh, I...my husband, Will, loved waffles and especially maple syrup. It ended up all over his face, too."

That was the first time Eleanor had said anything about her late husband in front of the men. She startled herself when she said his name, and while dabbing Ray's face just then, she felt a simple comfort she had sorely missed. She couldn't hold back the tears and excused herself from the table.

"He died quickly, not quite four years ago," Louise explained to Ray.

Then she looked over at Dirk and said, "He was the love of her life." When their eyes met, Louise dropped her chin and pushed her chair from the table. "I'll be back. Think I should check on Eleanor."

The men sat still, hands in their laps, appearing to have nothing to say. Ray lightened the mood. "Well, I don't know about you, but I could use a Bloody Mary." He motioned to the waiter.

"Make that two." Dirk held up two fingers.

"So," Ray began, "how are you doing with being around your ex-wife three times in a week?"

"You don't mince words, do you?" Dirk jabbed at his friend. "Well, it's nice. I've missed Louise. Didn't realize how much until now. But, man, I'm not stepping on your toes, nothing like that. It's just that we were together a long time, and well, you know, there's no ill-will between us."

"I can see that," Ray agreed, a pleased look on his face. "I wish I could be friends with my ex-wife, but she despises me. It's nice to see you get along with yours. It's really a shame that Eleanor lost her husband like that. She's a fine woman. But four years, hmm…I'm surprised she's not married again."

"Yeah, she's quite a catch…and so is my ex-wife. Just how much *do* you like Louise?"

"I like her a lot, she's…" Ray stopped talking seeing the ladies moving toward them.

"Bloody Mary's?" Louise shrieked, watching the waiter place the drinks on the table. "Great idea. I'll have one, as well. You?" she asked Eleanor who was now smiling and refreshed.

"You betcha!"

❦

The week went on as usual. Eleanor put a down payment on the cottage she had been considering and reported that she'd be moving in thirty days. Louise was sad to see her go, but glad to see her moving on and especially glad that she was staying in the Carolinas.

No more plans were made for the foursome to get together, and Louise mentioned that she had a date the following weekend. She didn't say with whom, but Eleanor assumed it was Ray.

Meanwhile, Dirk called Eleanor and asked if she'd be his

guest at a business party. His date had to cancel, and he
didn't want to go solo. He added that the meal was being
catered by the most prestigious restaurant in the city and no
one should miss out on such an opportunity. Knowing she'd
be stuck at home alone while Louise was out on the town,
she accepted.

The red dress she had bought looked better on the
mannequin than on herself, Eleanor decided. But the black
heels were perfect. Louise was already dressed and gone
when Eleanor came out of her bedroom looking more
ravishing than she had in years. She wondered what Louise
would think if she knew she was going out with Dirk. Why
she hadn't told her, she wasn't certain. But mature women
don't tell each other everything; a skill learned later in life.
There was a sophistication to being mysterious, and besides,
Louise wasn't married to Dirk anymore, and she now had
Ray, the only man since Will that made Eleanor heartily
laugh. *But he does that for everyone.* She stopped herself in mid-
thought and poured a glass of wine while she waited for
Dirk's arrival.

"You look quite the beauty," Dirk said when Eleanor
opened the door.

"And you look quite handsome," she said, pleased to see
Dirk wearing a suit. "The tie is fabulous!"

"Thank you." Dirk grinned and walked into the living
room, looking around for other signs of life. "Is Louise
here?"

"No, she's on a date tonight."

"Oh. With Ray?" he cocked his head, his look exposing a
bit more than simple curiosity.

"I'm not sure. She didn't say. Would you like a drink
before we go?"

"No thank you. I'd like to get there soon if you don't

mind." Dirk looked around the room again as if he was missing something and then again over his shoulder when they went out the door. Eleanor got the impression that he was hoping Louise would suddenly pop out from nowhere. She caught a disappointment in his expression and wanted to pat him on the back as if to console him. She had watched him and Louise getting to know each other again, and it was bittersweet knowing that Ray was such a nice guy and caught in the middle of it. Though Ray seemed to take it all in stride; the man was comfortable in his own skin, just like her Will.

Dirk was attentive at the party, introducing her to his co-workers, and making sure her glass was filled. They mingled and danced together and enjoyed each other's company. Afterwards, Eleanor invited him in for a night cap.

They sat at the kitchen table sharing a bottle of wine with leftover cheesecake. The alcohol kept the conversation light until Dirk brought up the subject of Louise. "You know, I regret having that affair."

"Oh?" Eleanor sat her glass down and eyed him thoughtfully. "Is that what broke you two up?" She hadn't known that part. Louise had always said that they had just gone separate ways.

"Yes," he sighed, "I was sorry as soon as it happened. Louise let me go pretty easily though. Neither of us fought for each other. Damn pride, I think."

"And now here you are back in each other's lives. How does that feel?"

"Hmmm," Dirk threw his head back, "feels nice, but boy is my timing bad."

"Oh, because of Ray?" Eleanor peered over her wine glass.

"He *is* a neat guy. She couldn't have picked anyone better. Don't you think? You seem to like him, too."

"Who wouldn't? He's, well, he's so much like my husband, Will, I'm kind of under his spell. Of course, I wouldn't tell Louise that. And if you don't mind, I'd rather you didn't either."

Dirk sat up straighter. "Sounds fair enough. I'd appreciate it if you wouldn't tell Louise or Ray how I feel either."

"Our secret," Eleanor leaned over and offered her pinky finger to Dirk. They locked fingers in a pact.

"I like you a lot, Eleanor. Thank you for going with me tonight."

"My pleasure. I like you, too, Dirk," she said, squeezing his finger before she let it go.

"I think we should seal our friendship with a kiss while this wine is doing all the talking for me." Dirk rose from his chair.

Eleanor stood up, and they met halfway. He put his hands around her waist.

"I agree," she smiled, eyes half closed. "It's been a while, so go gently."

"Of course," he said, placing his lips on hers, the mustache tickling her mouth, until he pressed harder, and the tickling instantly went away. It was a good kiss and Eleanor enjoyed it so much, she put her arms around his neck and encouraged it to last longer.

"Oh, are we disturbing something?" Louise's voice was heard from across the kitchen.

"I do believe we are," Ray said kiddingly, peeping out from behind her.

Eleanor quickly dropped her arms, and Dirk pulled his hands from her waist.

"You two look gorgeous," Ray said, reaching out to shake

Dirk's hand. "Hi, buddy. Good to see you. And you, too, Eleanor."

Eleanor felt her face blush even more. Ray was giving her that endearing impish look she was already so fond of.

Louise stood watching the scene with a raised eyebrow, and finally forced a smile when Dirk greeted her. She loosened her face and said, "Well, I hope you saved us some cheesecake. We've been out dancing, and I'm starving!"

Within seconds, shoes were kicked off and everyone sat around the table filling glasses with wine and devouring the rest of the dessert. Eleanor didn't like that she felt self-conscious, and looking over at Dirk, she hoped he didn't feel the same way. Leave it to Ray to start another one of his humorous anecdotes to slice through the edginess in the air. Within minutes, everyone was amused.

Halloween was just around the corner and Dirk's company was throwing a masquerade party in which a full face mask was required. The idea was to mimic the early sixteenth century Venetian Carnival and be unidentified behind the mask. Full costume was optional, but Louise had always loved dressing up for Halloween and her excitement rubbed off on Eleanor and Ray. The ladies raced to the costume store and spent an entire afternoon trying on elaborate gowns and masks, feathered hats, corsets, and scarves. With the trunk full, they drove home, giggling all the way.

The night of the party had arrived, and to make the event even more fun, they would arrive in a taxi, separately from Dirk and Ray. The ballroom was full of dashing men dressed in flowing pants or tights lined in gold trim, vests and billowy long-sleeved shirts, three-pronged hats, feathers galore. Some allowed their chests to be revealed, and Louise confessed that she loved studying them without being recognized. The women's gowns were so full, they had to lean over from the waist to whisper into each other's ears.

Eleanor was dazzled by the colors, gold, purple, silver dripping everywhere, decadent, and mysterious, as she walked slowly through the crowd, everyone bowing when they came upon one another, their extensive head dress grazing each other's. Hardly a voice was heard from those who wished to remain anonymous. Only Eleanor and Louise knew their identities behind their gawdy masks, each with a blue fake sapphire glued to the forehead. Everyone else, including Dirk and Ray were a mystery. The ladies went separate ways and planned to meet up later at the bar.

The orchestra played softly behind the scenes as the room filled, then lively music brought many to the dance floor. Emboldened behind the mask, Eleanor waded through them. Someone scooped her up and twirled her around and around so aggressively, she knew it wasn't Dirk, as she had danced with him before. But she had not danced with Ray. She strained to see the eyes behind the mask. Could it be him? She smiled, hoping it was, and then when the man clumsily dipped her, nearly dropping her on her head, she hoped it wasn't Ray. She couldn't stand the suspense any longer and asked, "Ray, is that you?"

"No, darling lady. I'm not, unless of course you want me to be." The stranger, in full acting mode for the era, pulled her dramatically into his arms and stared into her eyes. "Hmm, your eyes are most brilliant. Are you Deborah?"

"Not I," Eleanor answered, pulling away. She spotted Louise walking toward the bar. She waved goodbye to the man and just before she reached her, a man dashed over, took Louise by the hand, and led her to the far end of the room. Eleanor ordered a drink and observed them. After a while, they embraced and danced a slow waltz. "Darn it, she found Ray."

Eleanor turned away, partially lifted the mask and sipped the wine quickly. Now the game wouldn't be near as exciting without Ray in it. But where was Dirk? She surveyed the room, hoping to spot something familiar that might reveal him. It was hopeless.

The announcer came to the stage and got everyone's attention. "Now, my dear guests. Sometime in the next five minutes, the lights will go off and you will remove your mask and kiss the person you have selected. When I give the signal, the kiss will stop, the masks returned to your face, and no one will know the better. Unless of course, you wish to reveal yourself...which you may. Your decision. Now, place yourselves. You have very little time to locate the man or woman you will kiss."

Oohs, and aahs, and giggles all around, the lights began slowly dimming. Eleanor panicked and just when she was about to turn and run, someone came out of nowhere and took her hand. She could barely see his costume, and the glove he wore was soft as silk. The lights went completely out. It was too late, she had to play along. She slowly raised her mask and felt the stranger touch her chin, guiding her toward him. In the dark, they found each other's mouths. His lips were warm and inviting and his breath tasted sweet, like a fine bourbon; maple syrup crossed her mind. The kiss started small and delicate, then moved toward a deep passionate one as he pulled her closer, his hand holding hers now pressed upon her back, the other gently placed on her neck. Eleanor felt her body go limp.

Whoever was running the show had enough sense to gradually raise the lights so that everyone could slowly recover from what they had just done, their faces unseen or seen, they're choice, as it should be, after such intimacy with possibly a complete stranger.

Eleanor slowly pulled down her mask, once again incognito. When she looked out from behind it at the man, he had put his back on, too. She was disappointed when he turned and walked away. What a thrill! What a divine moment! She must know who that man was, even if it was Dirk's boss, or even if the stranger was married. Who cares? She could not go home with that incredible kiss on her lips and not attach a face to it. She felt faint, as she watched him disappear into the crowd.

She had not realized it, but when they were kissing, her grip on his hand was so tight that when he let go of her, the glove he wore slipped off his hand and into hers. She held it to her chest and went to find a seat. All those around were either openly laughing or hiding once again behind their masks. The game was a success, and everyone clapped in delight.

As the guests resumed dancing, Eleanor thought about Will, trying to remember his kisses. She could not remember them being as passionate as the one she had just experienced. He was beginning to fade and realizing that made her cry. She never wanted to forget the love of her life. The man who always made sure she laughed, even after the miscarriage, through the recession, through the deaths of friends and family, there was always room for laughter. She snapped out of it when someone tapped her on the shoulder.

"Hey, are you ready to call it a night?" Louise had removed her mask and was leaning down close to her. "I'm not sure I can take another minute in this girdle."

"Sure, sure. I think I need to freshen up in the lady's

room before I take off my mask. I'll see you outside." She stuffed the glove inside her purse.

The restroom was crowded, and alive with chatter. Eleanor squeezed in between the women all lined up in front of the mirror powdering their noses and applying more lipstick. Her face was blotched, and anyone could see that she had been crying. She pressed a cold wet paper towel on her eyes and reapplied her make-up. It was hard to feel sad with so much liveliness in the snug room. The women were as lightheaded as teenage girls.

Refreshed and ready to join her friends, Eleanor walked out into the cool night air. She stood quietly unnoticed off to the side looking up at the stars and thinking how that one incredible kiss had somehow revived a sense of herself that she had long ago buried. It was at that precise moment she glanced behind her and saw her own shadow. "I found you," she whispered to the muted image, imagining that it was smiling back at her.

Across the way, she saw Louise talking to a man, his back turned toward her. When Louise spotted Eleanor, she waved. The man looked over his shoulder and waved, too. It was Ray. Dirk pulled up in his car just when she greeted them.

"The boys are giving us a ride home," Louise grinned, struggling with her dress as she climbed into the front seat. Ray helped her gather up all the fabric and carefully shut the car door. He did the same for Eleanor. Stuffed in the car, their hats shedding feathers in the air, they made fun of themselves all the way home.

"You must come in for drinks," Louise insisted. "We have to talk more about tonight. Wasn't it divine?"

Dirk looked at Ray, and they both nodded a yes.

"Don't take off those hats yet, I want to get a picture," Louise ordered and pranced inside the house.

"Be funnier if she took the pictures *after* we take these hats off. I bet my hair is stuck to my head like a drowned rat," Ray joked.

"An *old* drowned rat," Dirk said dryly.

"Well, I'll be darn, there's some hope for you after all, buddy ole boy." Ray punched Dirk in the arm playfully, and they entered the house arm in arm.

Drinks all around, the four friends took selfies on the sofa and laughed until they couldn't breathe and laughed even more when Ray removed his hat. Rescuing him from the onslaught of ridicule, Eleanor led him to her bathroom where she plopped him down on a vanity chair and went after his smashed and sweaty hair with a blow dryer. He even allowed her to part his hair on the opposite side and let an errant curl dangle just above his eye. But no matter how hard she tried she couldn't get the cowlick to stay down.

"OK, so who played the light's out game tonight at the party?" Ray asked, re-entering the living room. "And don't say a word about my hair." He sat down on the floor and scanned the onlookers muffling their laughter.

"I played it." Louise giggled.

Eleanor looked over at Ray expecting one of his naughty grins, but he kept his expressions to himself. She took a chance and teased, "I bet *I* know who kissed you, Louise."

"Oh really?" Louise' interest piqued. "So, who do you think it was, Eleanor?"

"Well, I thought it was you, Ray," Eleanor said, feeling a little foolish after he didn't respond, his expression still unreadable.

"What about you, Dirk?" Eleanor turned her attention from Ray.

"It was me Louise was kissing. I thought she knew." Dirk looked disappointed.

Louise took a long drink of wine, avoided Dirk's eyes, and looked directly at Ray. "And you, Ray?"

"Of course, I played. I don't know who she was, but I tell you what, she was a fabulous kisser."

"Oh, so I bet you wished she had revealed herself, eh Ray?" Louise chided.

Ray didn't have a joke ready this time and chose silence.

All heads turned to Eleanor. "What about you, El?"

"Yeah, what about you?" Ray nudged her leg with his elbow.

"I fell in love," Eleanor said dreamily, the wine allowing her to talk freely. "The guy that picked me kissed me like I've never been kissed before. A maple syrup kiss," she sighed. "Matter of fact, it was so nice, I forgot all about Will. Made me cry."

"Oh, El," Louise leaned over and patted her on the back. "We've got to find out who that man was."

Dirk spoke up, "And just how would you do that? Could be anyone, could be a married man, could be, shoot, who knows? What are the odds?"

Eleanor leaned over and picked up her purse. "It could be easier than you think." She pulled out the glove and held it in the air. "I have this. It slipped off his hand."

Ray crossed his legs and sat up straighter, an unusual seriousness on his face. "Maybe you should just keep the glove and the kiss as a fond memory. You could be very disappointed if you find him."

"That's true, Eleanor," Louise said. She put her hand on Dirk's knee and lovingly squeezed it. "I'm not disappointed, Dirk. I'm really not."

Dirk smiled. Ray smiled. Eleanor smiled, too. It's wonderful being this age, Eleanor thought as she looked around at her mature friends. Egos were put aside, and an appreciation for one another and their individual selves filled their hearts. It took years of facing life's ups and downs to get to this kind of gentle understanding. Seasoned, was the word she was looking for.

They finished off another round of drinks and talked until after midnight.

"You boys cannot drive home tonight," Louise declared. "One of you take the sofa in here, the other gets a blow-up mattress in my office."

"No argument here," Dirk said, followed by a loud satisfying yawn as he stood waiting for instructions.

"I'll take the sofa in here. Just a pillow is all I need," Ray said, throwing his body face-down on the cushion. "Never slept in tights before," he mumbled, "this is a first."

Eleanor kissed both men on their cheeks and said goodnight, while Louise made up a bed for Dirk and threw a pillow from the hallway at Ray.

Sometime later, Ray was lying on his back wide awake, thinking about the woman he had kissed at the party. He saw a shadow moving down the hallway, and soon after, two huddled figures tiptoeing in the dark. He exhaled a long thoughtful sigh.

Eleanor was on her side hugging a pillow, reliving the kiss, and the feeling she hoped she could preserve when someone slightly opened her bedroom door, stepped in, and oh so quietly closed it. She held her breath.

The dappled effect from the moon shining through the trees led the lone figure to where she was facing. Kneeling down beside her, he gently placed the matching glove on her cheek. Knowing then who it was, Eleanor let out a tiny giggle and took the other glove from underneath her pillow. She ran it across his lips and pulled Ray into her arms in a welcoming hug.

"Sleeping on the sofa is killing my back," he groaned in her ear. "Would you mind if I sleep with you? I'll be a gentleman, I promise."

When he began moving his body onto the bed she whispered, "Not in *my* bed."

"What?" Ray reared back and tried to catch the expression on her face. "Dirk is in Louise' bed."

"Of course, he is. But you are *not* sleeping with me in *that* costume."

"Wouldn't think of it," he blurted, first stripping off the shirt before tackling the tights. He looked so ridiculous trying to remove them, teetering back and forth, cursing under his breath when he hit his toe on a chair, Eleanor burst out laughing. Then Ray laughed, and soon they heard laughing from Louise' bedroom.

"Go to sleep, kids!" Louise playfully yelled, timely followed by Dirk's deep demanding voice. "Don't make me get the hose!"

Surprised by Dirk's spontaneous and witty comeback and the whole ludicrous situation unfolding, Ray bellowed out a throaty horselaugh and dropped to the floor where he tried to shimmy out of the tights. "My god," he grunted with each tug, "it's alive, and it's strangulating me! Hurry, get some scissors!"

Eleanor slipped off the bed onto her knees and attempted to help him. She was laughing so hard she lost grip of the elastic as it slapped back into place and clung firmly to his thick thighs. "It's not...it's not budging!" she cried.

"Call the fire department!" Ray managed to say, gagging on the words.

Giving up, Eleanor flopped down next to him; both collapsing on their backs with uncontrollable guffaws.

45

Finally relieved of the costume, Ray inhaled deeply, leaned over Eleanor, and watched her trying to catch her breath, her eyes closed, her hands crossed over her rapidly beating heart, a gratifying smile parting her wet lips. He waited for her eyes to open. This time he wanted her to see the man who was giving her a maple syrup kiss.

THERE WAS YOU

*L*et's not go," Gloria whined, leaning across the car seat, squeezing Nelson's arm tightly enough to make him look in her direction.

"What do you mean, let's not go?" he asked irritably, trying to read her expression in the dark, knowing better than to take his eyes off the road while driving in such a heavy downpour. The splashing rain against the windshield reflecting on her pale face made her look like a sinister old woman lurking behind a jaggedly sheer black veil. He wondered at that very moment why he had ever been attracted to her.

"Well, first of all, the party will be full of pretentious women, and I don't even want to say what you already know about your men friends, and if we go, you'll get drunk which will give you the liberty to flirt with every female there who will be all over you anyway because you were so popular in college, and before you know it, I'll be glaring across the room at you or you'll be staring me down with that fake smile of yours, and when we finally realize it's time to leave

47

we'll be so mad at each other, one of us will lock ourselves in the bathroom or take off in the car, leaving the other behind and by morning we will have built up so much hate from a bad-night's sleep that we'll spend the week not talking until finally you say, *I'm sorry* and not remembering exactly why, just knowing that whatever *you* did was not good for me, and we'll try to shake it off and treat each other nice like it's the end of the world, followed up by a lot, I mean *a lot* of make-up sex, and I'll wear you totally out, and then you'll say something stupid and then…"

"Don't say another word, Gloria…I'm turning around."

Ten minutes later they were back in their apartment, Gloria humming a little tune while mixing her favorite Absolute and soda with three twists of lemon, while Nelson glumly carried a bottle of Jameson and a shot glass to the sofa. Their shoes were kicked off by the door, Gloria in her bare feet, Nelson in his nylon socks.

Gloria sat down next to her boyfriend. "Now isn't this nice just the two of us," she cooed, leaning in for a kiss. Nelson turned away and took a swig of his drink.

"What's the matter?" she asked, as if nothing had taken place, and they were simply settling down for a quiet evening at home.

"It's just that, well, I wanted to go to that party." He slumped further into the sofa and sulked.

"I can't even imagine why. Those people are such snobs, and I would have been so bored, which is another reason why we would have ended up in a fight."

"My best friend, James was supposed to be there. I haven't seen him in a year, and the guys said he was only coming into town for this one night, and now, I won't get to see him at all."

Crunching loudly on the ice in her drink, Gloria's

thoughts drifted back to their last fight. They had been at the bar where Nelson's college buddies hung out and in walked his ex-girlfriend, Pam. Gloria remembered observing all eyes in the place turning Pam's direction and then darting across the room to catch Nelson's response as he watched his old flame enter the bar.

"They were quite the item," the woman next to Gloria insisted on sharing. "I never thought anything could pry them loose," she added, looking smugly down at Gloria as if she had by sheer luck won the biggest stuffed animal at the fair.

Gloria remembered everything around her turning black. Like a lizard with eyes on each side of its head, one eye scrutinized every move Pam made, and the other stayed on Nelson as he stood at the bar ordering their drinks, his head bowed, clearly trying to concentrate only on the task at hand. And just as Gloria feared, Pam spotted Nelson and eased through the crowd toward him. It took every ounce of energy Gloria had to keep from racing to his side and claiming her property. Instead, she stood back in the shadows and watched, like a hawk eyeing its prey.

Certain that the hug when they greeted one another lasted much too long, and when Pam let her hand linger on Nelson's shoulder while she was obviously soliciting sex, Gloria felt a familiar rage implode. She marched straight over to the bar, picked up the drink that should have been in her hand by now, and tossed it in Pam's face. Nelson stiffened, mouth gaping, and finally when he was able to loosen his shocked expression, he apologized to Pam, grabbed Gloria by the arm and dragged her kicking and screaming toward the exit.

The fight between them lasted all week, the longest one yet, and was never resolved, and now Gloria would cunningly revive it. "Who you *really* want to see is Pam, isn't it?" she asked in a sly accusatory voice.

"Why, so you can throw another drink in her face? Look, I just said I wanted to see James." Nelson placed his glass on the coffee table and braced himself for another lashing. Avoiding eye contact that usually flipped her switch, he cowered and imagined himself on his knees facing a guillotine. Just before the blade fell, he conjured up James in chain mail and plate armor wielding a sword larger than his short stubby body could carry, ramming through the crowd to rescue him. When he felt Gloria's devilish eyes boring a hole into the side of his head, he let go of the fantasy, turned on the television, and silently prayed for a distraction.

The next morning, Nelson was relieved waking up to an empty side of the bed, until he found Gloria asleep on the sofa, surrounded by pictures of girls cut out from his high school yearbook, all desecrated with hateful words like "slut", "whore", "cocksucker" and "cow" written in red ink across their virgin faces. He quietly dressed and left the scene, not returning until late that evening.

In a short skirt and low-neck blouse, Gloria greeted a subdued Nelson at the door with her practiced smile. The living room had been emptied of all clues that something ugly had taken place the night before. *The Sweetest Taboo* played softly in the background and candles were lit throughout. The thick syrupy aroma made Nelson's eyes water.

Gloria gingerly led him to a seat at the kitchen table. She

dropped to her knees and removed his shoes. Slowly slithering up his body, she grabbed his face and rubbed it into her glittered cleavage. Intent on teasing him, she pulled away, sashayed to the kitchen, and slipped on a pair of oven mitts.

Digging out flakes of glitter from his nostrils, Nelson watched her warily as she placed the enchiladas with peas frozen entrée in front of him. The candlelight dancing across her face reminded him again of the old lady beneath a veil, now gradually appearing more like an ugly witch. He shuddered, not realizing how distorted his own face had become until Gloria spoke, "What's the matter? You look sick."

"I guess, I guess my mind went elsewhere," he said weakly. Quickly stuffing a spoonful of half-cooked peas in his mouth, he muttered an insincere apology. Before she could ask where his thoughts had gone, he pretended to choke and spewed the peas across the table.

"Gross!" Gloria reared back and threw her napkin at Nelson. "Well, just keep your mind on me, baby," she insisted, gripping his thigh, and turning her head in disgust as a slimy pea slowly dripped down the candle.

A nervous sigh of relief trickled from Nelson's mouth. He imagined himself as the invisible man, slowly removing his bandages and disappearing out of sight. By the skin of his teeth, he had successfully avoided another fight.

As they often did, they barely touched the meal, guzzled the wine, and passed up dessert, advancing to the bedroom, Gloria leading the way.

Nelson dreamed of the veiled woman that night and woke up the next morning in an uncomfortable hangover sweat next to his bed partner. He felt like he'd been punched in the stomach. How in the world had he let this woman who had the sexual energy of an entire cheerleader squad move in and bring with her a green-eyed monster that came out in full color when he least expected it? Like the time at the grocery store, when he glanced at a magazine with a sexy woman on the cover begging the reader to open her pages, Gloria pushed the grocery cart into the back of his legs, causing him to buckle to the floor. And there was a crazy scene at a restaurant when a female colleague from work dropped by their table. After a few friendly exchanges she left Nelson in Gloria's jealous grip, kicking him repeatedly under the table, and finally, when not getting the answers from him that would suit her, she emptied the entire saltshaker over his plate of food.

Anything could ignite the jealous demon inside her, and he knew that Green-eyed Monster Gloria had to go. But every time he made the slightest suggestion that she move out, she would freak out so badly he would have to lock himself in the bathroom until she grew tired of pounding on the door. It could have been much worse if not for the pile of reading material he kept next to the toilet.

To make matters even more complicated, in those few minutes at the bar that he had alone with Pam, before Gloria doused her with booze, he realized that he was still in love with his ex-girlfriend. He was certain that he could see in her eyes that she loved him, too. And here he was, a fool stuck with this crazy female, afraid to tell her the truth. Spineless and defeated, he felt trapped, on a hamster wheel to nowhere.

❧❧

Gloria worked during the day as a bartender. On this particular day, she had been asked to work the late-night shift. Thrilled to have a free evening alone, Nelson took the opportunity to see a band he liked, and one that Gloria loathed.

It felt surreal walking into the small, charming setting, standing against the wall, a cold beer in hand, enjoying the music among like-minded fans. When the lights dimmed, everyone knew a song with meaning was about to be played, and the room grew silent. The lyrics pierced Nelson's heart:

You've got the key to my house
Key to my car
Money for trips stuffed in a big glass jar
Toothbrush in my bathroom
Panties on the floor
A big pile of love notes from the pillow to the drawer
I turned around just to watch the moon
Suddenly baby there was you
Right in my face, all over the place
There was you.

Truer words had never been sung when in the middle of the song Nelson felt his body slump against the wall.

But honey you don't have the key to my heart
You never did, right from the start
How did this happen you just slipped right on in
I didn't see it coming…the original sin
You said with a wink in your eye
I'll change you for the better, a more perfect guy
But what's a guy to do when he's not in love with you

As the lyrics clarified his current situation, he knew he could not spend another day with Gloria. He purchased the band's CD and while driving to the bar where she worked, he was emboldened by the song as he played it over and over, preparing to finally free himself from the clutches of the green-eyed monster.

Inside the bar, he had not expected it to be so large and quite so dark. A six-piece band was on stage. Wall-to-wall people gathered, chatting so noisily he had to yell his order to the waitress. He was hiding behind the sound man and all his fancy equipment when he spotted Gloria taking orders at the far end of the bar, easygoing in her role, without a trace of her true identity on her smiling face. Nelson felt his courage waning.

He tried imagining himself walking on stage, standing boldly in front of the microphone, and announcing to the audience that he was breaking up with Gloria. The men would applaud with triumphant cheers and carry him around the room on their shoulders. The women would fight over who would be his next girlfriend. Meanwhile, the bouncer would usher the screaming unhinged Gloria outside where she would be tied to the hood of her car like a dead deer. Oh, if only.

The second beer had him rethinking the situation. What could he possibly accomplish with the music and loud talkers drowning out his words? And even if he did tell her now, she'd eventually arrive at his place where it would be impossible to escape her wrath. Already defeated, he slipped outside unnoticed and into the parking lot to carefully weigh his options.

Inside his car, he reclined the seat and sat numbly singing the words from the song, "I turned around just to tie my shoes, suddenly baby there was you, right in my face, all over the place, there was you…"

His singing was interrupted by the voices of people pouring out the back door heading toward their parked cars.

The place was obviously closing. He waited for everyone to leave, and just when he decided to go inside and have the talk with Gloria, she came walking out arm-in-arm with a flaming-red-bearded man, sporting a super-sized cowboy hat on his head. Nelson slid further down into the seat and observed.

When they reached Gloria's car, the man lifted her up and plopped her down on the hood and the kissing began. Oh boy, did they ever kiss! While the man's hands roamed up and down Gloria's fish-net stockings, she removed his hat and wildly ran her fingers through his long hair.

Nelson felt a sudden streak of jealousy race through him and before it took hold, he shook it loose, got out of the car and walked over to the couple who had not heard him approaching, too wrapped up in smooching to care. At a suitable distance, he stopped and imagined himself as a tree trunk, standing perfectly still, grounded, and waiting for whatever cruel force of nature would be thrust upon him. I can do this, I can do this, he repeated to himself.

When Gloria finally took a breather and looked over her kissing partner's shoulder, her eyes narrowed spotting Nelson standing there, expressionless, arms folded.

"What is it?" the man pushed away and followed Gloria's gaze. "Whatcha need, Mister?" he asked, slapping the ten-gallon hat back on his mussed hair.

"Not a thing. I just came here to talk to Gloria. Do you mind?"

Gloria slipped off the hood of the car, tearing her stockings on the bumper grid, and after a few choice curse words, she calmly walked over to Nelson and said, "What's up?"

Taken aback by her mild approach, as if nothing unusual was happening, and by the guileless look of curiosity on the man's face, softened by the lipstick smear around his mouth, Nelson stood there feeling foolish, his bottom lip hanging.

"Well, you didn't come all the way over here after midnight to stand there with your foot in your mouth, did you?" Gloria put her hands on her hips as if she were talking to a teenage boy who had just got caught putting the empty milk carton back in the refrigerator.

Still intimidated by the little woman with the fierce libido, he managed a submissive, "No." Stiffening up, he looked over at the man and announced, "I'd like to speak to Gloria in private, if you please."

"Up to my wife, here," he tossed a thumb toward Gloria.

"Wife?" Nelson gulped, thrusting his head forward.

"We're separated," Gloria announced nonchalantly.

"You never said a word about a *husband*," Nelson said, clearly dumbfounded, jerking his head back in place.

"Gabe, meet Nelson, my roommate."

Gabe put his hand out and slid forward, dragging his boots through the crunching gravel, like a rooster gearing up for a cockfight. "Howdy," he said, gruffly.

Nelson instinctively put his hand out, and Gabe squeezed it so hard, he nearly buckled under his grip. "Uh, well, then I guess what I have to say will matter to both of you. So, here goes," he said, stepping back in a defensive mode, "Gloria, I'd like for you to move out. I'd like for you to move out tomorrow."

"Oh, you would, would you?" she stepped forward with a cocky swagger, her head bobbing. "Just because you caught me kissing my own husband?"

Nelson looked confused. "No, well, no, not really. I mean, well, NO! Because I don't love you, Gloria. I think we're wasting each other's time."

"Really?" she dragged out the word and rolled her eyes.

"What does love got to do with it anyway? It's really because you still want Pam. Admit it, you, shallow creep!"

"That's not…"

"Oh, *please*. Everyone knows it. You even said her name in your sleep last night. Didn't you even feel me punch you?"

"I did? You punched me?"

"Yes, to both, so give me a break and tell me really why you want me out."

Nelson placed his hand on his sore stomach. *So that's why it hurts.* Adding another offense to the long list, he knew if he spelled out the awful things about Gloria that she would explode, and he'd cower, and they'd go right back to the madness. Instead, all that he could say was, "Because of the old woman in the veil."

Gloria squinted over at Gabe. Gabe squinted back. Simultaneously they turned to Nelson, a confused look on their faces demanding an explanation.

"Yeah, well, there's this woman in a black veil that's been appearing in my head lately. I can't explain it, but I think it's you, the real you behind that veil, and you're telling me to let you go. So, that's what I'm doing." The explanation, as bizarre as it sounded was the best he could offer, and he felt immediate satisfaction saying it out loud, even if was under a bug-filled lamp light in a dusty parking lot in front of Cowboy Gabe.

Nelson sensed Gabe posing for a fight when he sucked in his gut, slid his fingers along the rim of his wide-brimmed hat, and spit on the ground. He reared back, pointed his finger in the air and said with some earnest, "You know dude, I kind of understand what you're saying. I've seen that woman in the veil myself when me and Gloria were living together and had all those nasty fights. She was one ugly, mean-looking gal, and I thought I was losing my mind, but now that you've seen her, too, well..."

"What ARE you talking about, you IDIOT?" Gloria faced Gabe with balled-up fists and began to berate him the way she had slaughtered Nelson's ego so many times in their short life together. Her words flew from her mouth like bats flying out from under the South Congress bridge at dusk. Knowing it would take her quite a while to empty everything in her head, Nelson slowly inched backwards to his car. Gloria was so wound up, she hadn't even noticed him leaving until she saw his taillights round the corner, the end of a song blaring from the opened windows, "only me, there was only me, no compromise, no telling me lies, only me, there was only me..."

As it happened, with Gabe's help, Gloria did move out the next day. Either Gabe was the kind of man that could tolerate a woman like her, or by the looks of the shiner on his left eye, Gloria had beaten him into submission. No matter, the relief Nelson felt while watching them pack her car – a safe bird's eye view through the second story window of a café across the street – assured him that he had done the right thing. He had the locksmith there in no time flat, thus ending an embarrassing chapter of his life.

With many sincere apologies, a lot of ass kissing, and finally promising to never again see or talk about Gloria, Nelson convinced Pam to pick up where they had left off. The marquise-cut diamond engagement ring he placed on her finger would surely grease the way to forgiveness. His best friend, James flew in to celebrate, and a party was planned for the whole gang to meet up.

The party was held at a Greek restaurant, a perfectly friendly setting for a reunion. A tall-backed, U-shaped booth was reserved just for Nelson and Pam and James. There was much to catch up on and the seating arrangement would allow them some privacy from the others while they exchanged stories. Nelson and Pam had arrived first and placed themselves in the back of the booth, saving room for James and others should they stop by to chat.

"James has something important to share with us," Nelson told Pam as they sipped their martinis.

"Oh, really? He's been back for only a week, and he's already got something important to share? Curious," Pam winked, "I wonder who she is."

"James? Ha, ha! Unlikely. He's a sworn bachelor if ever there was one, and I think he likes food more than women. His dad did tell me he might be moving back here, but that's a secret, so act surprised when he tells us. He's a sensitive thing, you know."

"Like you?" Pam winked again, and when Nelson moved in for a kiss, someone abruptly slid into the booth beside him. Snapping their lips shut the couple turned their heads to see who it was.

Nelson saw James first; a nervous grin stretched between his pudgy cheeks as if he had just said something idiotic. Then he glanced over at Pam whose smile had turned to a scowl, now frozen in place. Following her glare, he reluctantly looked over his shoulder to see who James had brought to their table.

"Hi, Nelson," the woman purred, like a cat who had just dropped a dead mouse at his feet. "You never told me your friend James was so darn cute, and single on top of it!"

Nelson's entire face wilted upon seeing the old lady behind the veil.

"What's the matter? You look sick," Gloria said. Reaching behind her, she grabbed James' double chin and pointing it Nelson's direction, she reiterated, "Doesn't he look sick, honey? He sure looks sick to me."

Pinned to the back of the booth, Nelson imagined himself like Gumby, a flattened-out piece of soft clay slipping off the seat and underneath the table, crawling away unscathed. No such luck!

Pam squeezed Nelson's thigh with a grip that made his eyes water. She held tightly to the martini, armed and ready for just the right moment to toss it in the green-eyed monster's face.

THE BETTER MAN

A foggy and gray day was fitting for a man drained of all emotion. Pete felt as worthless as the bruised and rotten banana sitting on the floor of his pick-up truck. He had not meant to leave it there when he went inside the hospital. He had not meant to ignore the receptionist when she gave him a perky hello. Nor had he meant to fall asleep still clutching his wife's hand after she mumbled her final words: "You will forgive me, Pete. I know you will."

Only Pete had not realized it was her last breath until a nurse gently woke him and in a soothing voice suggested that he go to the front desk and notify family that Glenda Anne Pickett had died.

⌖

It was a set of unfortunate circumstances that had brought Pete and Glenda together. This is their story.

. . .

In the historic town of Good Hollow, the leaves from the Autumn Purple ash tree in Pete's backyard had fallen overnight, as if someone had blown a whistle and ordered it so. As he did every year, he would let the beautiful leaves remain on the ground until they were drained of all color. Fall was his favorite time of year, a calming period after a long hot summer of water activities. Pete owned a popular water sports store along the riverbank in an ideal spot to teach kayaking and rent out tubes to tourists and locals toting cold beer in coolers, returning only when they were burnt and satisfactorily intoxicated, a gradual process that usually took about four hours. The lazy fall season would also give him more time to focus on fixing up his home in preparation for the next phase of his life, which he hoped would include a wife and family.

Tinkering in the garage was something Pete enjoyed every Saturday morning while waiting for the next football game to fill the rest of the day. That six-pack chilling in the refrigerator and brats soaking in beer thrilled him every time. For a healthy-minded single man, it couldn't get any better than this, unless he could get that old 1967 Mustang in the shed up and running. Pete had chosen a simple but satisfying life, safe from the cruel world outside of his small-town surroundings.

Back in the high school days, Big Al, they called Alan Smith because he had a broad back like a steam shovel and hands to match, was not only Pete's best friend, but also Glenda's boyfriend. The three of them were thick as thieves in their senior year. But when all that hoopla was over, and Glenda and Big Al took off to college, Pete was drawn to the river and stayed behind.

Shortly after Glenda left Good Hollow, her mother abruptly divorced her father and moved to New York to marry another man. And not just any man – she married Big Al's father. Blindsided by this startling event, Glenda was forced into the awkward realization that Alan, her boyfriend, was now her stepbrother. The young couple soon split ways and rumor had it that the relationship ended in an embarrassing hush.

To make things worse for Glenda, she had to give up her final year of college and return to Good Hollow to tend to her lonely and terminally ill father and eventually to manage his meager estate. Poor Glenda had not only lost her boyfriend and her father, but she also lost the will to finish school and get her degree.

That's when Pete had stepped in. He saw an opportunity to make Glenda his own, and he wasn't about to pass it up. She had been hard to convince that he was the man for her, not a lick of college, and nothing like his buddy, Big Al, the most popular jock in high school from a prominently wealthy family.

Determined to ease her pain and to get Big Al out of her heart, he followed her around like a puppy dog, bending to her every whim. After several months of heavy petting and consoling, he persuaded Glenda to marry him.

As for Big Al, it was Glenda who insisted that they no longer communicate. The selfish part of Pete felt right about her decision but cutting Big Al out of his life wasn't easy. He loved the guy. The last time Pete saw his buddy was at a friend's wedding. Dressed to the nines in a tailored blue suit that expertly outlined his chiseled physique and enhanced his flaming red hair, Big Al had all the single women falling at his feet. While observing the charade, Pete was convinced that his pampered and worldly friend had survived just fine without Glenda. Maybe they could all be friends again, he hoped. Besides, Big Al showed no signs of animosity and seemed genuinely happy for them both.

But that night at the wedding reception watching the two of them dance together, Pete wondered if his wife had regretted not marrying the big bruiser. He tried not to let it bother him until when everyone was leaving, Big Al kissed her out in the dark parking lot. Pete only saw them pull away, and he never knew whether Glenda kissed him back or not.

Although hesitantly, Pete agreed to the four three-week-long trips his wife took that year to visit her mother in New York. The fact that her mother's husband paid for the flights made it easier. Plus, the best thing about Glenda's leaving was that when she returned, she was ravenous for sex. She was the aggressor, he the slave, and it would last for about three days and then drop off like a leak that had been sealed. He would have to wait patiently until her next trip to be satisfied again. And like clockwork, the day of departure arrived.

On the way to the airport, Glenda sat quietly staring out the car window, while Pete listened intently to the radio. "Hey, remember our neighbor's obnoxious retriever? The dog we named Private Sniff-a-lot because he couldn't keep his nose out of people's crotches. Well, the old boy broke his leg. Poor thing."

Stone-faced, Glenda gazed beyond the trees at the horizon with no response.

Pete reached over and cupped her knee in his hand, as he had done many times before.

"Oh!" Glenda jerked, looking down at his hand. "I'm sorry, I guess I was busy thinking."

"You've been drifting off like that a lot lately. Is everything alright? Is your mother alright?"

"She is. I mean, why wouldn't she be?" Glenda huffed.

"She's got plenty of money, everything she wants, the perfect life."

"I see. You're thinking about your dad, aren't you?"

"I suppose I was. It's his birthday tomorrow, and I was remembering how excited he got every year when my mother made his favorite Pineapple Upside-Down cake. Only, Mom didn't make it. Have I told you this before?"

"Yes, you told me that your aunt would come over and bake it, and your mother would take the credit."

"Yeah, I was just thinking what a lie that was and other lies I remember hearing all that year before mom took off with Mr. Fancy Smith of New York. She really broke my dad's heart, you know."

"Honey, we've been over this many times. I know it still hurts, losing your dad so early in life. But, honestly Glenda, it wasn't your mother's fault. People change, things happen. At least she waited until you left the nest before she divorced him."

"Oh, there you go again, ironing it all out so perfectly. I suppose next you're going to say that my marrying you instead of finishing college was the right thing to do. You know, I could have graduated this year."

"Are you saying that I took advantage of you?" Pete eased off the accelerator and waited for Glenda's answer.

'Well…maybe. I mean, I was depressed. And I was so mad at my mother. Dad would have been furious with me if he'd known I hadn't gone back to school. And Alan…"

"Alan never came back to see you even once. I know, I was there while you suffered. Me, ole sensitive Pete, holding up Big Al's girl. Well, as far as I'm concerned, the better man won."

Glenda turned her head to look out the window, and her cold silence brought tears to Pete's eyes. Determined not to put words in his wife's mouth, as he often did, he knew she would not give him the answer he so badly wanted. He also knew he would go home and sulk while Glenda would forget all about it, running compulsively through the streets of the Big Apple with her mother in high heels insisting that they enter every shop along the way, ending up with arms full of purchases at five-star restaurants perusing fancy menus with exotic drinks. That would have been Glenda's life if she and Big Al had not split up. He couldn't imagine how she could possibly trade in the river life with all its serenity for the hustle and bustle of that crazy, dirty city. In many ways, Pete felt as though he had saved Glenda's life. It never occurred to him until now that perhaps he had taken advantage of the situation.

"You don't have to come in with me this time, Pete. Just drop me off at the terminal. I only brought one bag. Mother insisted that she wanted to buy me a winter wardrobe, so I'll be coming home with more than I'm leaving with."

"But I love seeing you to the gate. Sure you don't want me to come in?" Pete looked longingly at Glenda who was now avoiding his eyes and digging in her purse for the flight information.

"It's OK, really, just pull in here," she said with a smile, pointing at the curb.

Glenda's smile was enough to make Pete dizzy, and that's all he needed to set himself back on track. He pulled over to the curb, jumped out of the car, and opened the trunk. The suitcase was stuffed and puffed at the seams. "What'd you have in here, our neighbor's dog?"

"No silly, just some of my childhood photos and old videos my mother asked for that she had left with dad," she explained, grabbing hold of the handle and yanking it onto the sidewalk.

Pete slammed the trunk closed and stood facing her.

"Well," she said, flashing that gorgeous smile again, "are you going to kiss me goodbye, or what?"

Pete offered her his biggest grin and scooped her up in his arms. "I'll love you forever, Glenda Anne." Then he kissed her hard and long until Glenda absentmindedly dropped her purse onto the cement. "There! Take that to New York, and remember where it came from, baby."

Glenda pulled back and bit hard on her lip. "I will," she said softly, the bottom of her eyelids dampening. "See you later." She grabbed her belongings and walked away.

Pete leaned against the car and watched her enter the building. *Turn around, Glenda. Turn around, damn it.*

Just before the glass door closed behind her, she looked over her shoulder and smiled. Relieved, Pete exhaled and carried that image with him all the way back home.

⚑⚑

The first week of Glenda's absence made Pete unusually restless. Her gleaming smile at the airport could not hide the sadness in her eyes. He felt the need to hear her voice. But with every call there was no answer. Unable to stay focused, he was determined to find out what was bothering her, so he packed a bag and drove the twelve-hour drive to New York.

Fall in New England entices folks from all over the country to the spectacular turning of the leaves along the highways and lazy winding roads. Pete noticed that even the ugly homes, worn and dilapidated, looked almost beautiful framed in golden red, brilliant orange, and intense purple foliage. With the windows rolled down, the earthy smell brought on a melancholy nostalgia until he reached the dreaded New Jersey Turnpike. From there he tightly gripped the steering wheel and finally relaxed when he saw New York City fading in his rear-view mirror.

Pete slowly pulled up to the massive wrought iron gate with the big S carved in gold. He remembered Glenda telling him that her mother's home was surrounded by fifty acres of rich forestland. Looking ahead he saw that the narrow road gently curved and disappeared inside a thicket of trees.

He jumped out of the truck to open the gate. It was locked. Across the road was a quaint café. He parked his vehicle next to the *Dew Drop In* sign and left it there.

Pete enjoyed climbing up the tall gate and jumping to the ground on the other side. He felt like a kid sneaking into an apple orchard. As he headed down the long drive, he began to feel uneasy anticipating what was around each corner. He wished that someone in the household was expecting him.

When he reached the home situated on a hill in all its estate majesty, he stopped and gawked. Glenda's description of her stepfather's home was nothing like this. It was much bigger than he had imagined and the closer he got, the smaller he felt. Another large S was neatly carved in wood and milled perfectly in the middle of two double doors. He spotted the doorbell button to his right and not realizing that he was shaking, he pressed it. Stepping back, hands clasped, he waited. He pressed the button again. Not a sound was heard from the other side, so he decided to walk around to the back of the home. There, he found a large, covered patio with enough outdoor furniture to fill three homes the size of his own. Tall plate glass windows lined up along the back wall and Pete could see the furnishings inside: grand sofas and tall wingback chairs, marble end tables, and a coffee table the size of a coffin. Lights were turned off, and it appeared quite uninhabited.

"Hmmm." Pete took off his baseball cap and scratched his head. An unexpected yawn tumbled out of his mouth. Realizing that he was tired from driving overnight with only two hours of sleep in the cab of his truck, he settled into one of the chaise lounges and sunk deep into its cushions. It wasn't long before the cool breeze wooed him into a bottomless slumber.

Glenda arrived shortly after. She gently removed the sleeping child from the car seat and carried her into the house and up the winding staircase to a room that had been specifically designed in varied shades of pink for a four-year-old girl. Lowering her slowly to avoid waking the sleeping beauty, she tucked her in and lightly kissed her forehead. Staring down at the little girl, she marveled at her remarkable beauty. Then she tiptoed out of the room and hurried back down the stairs to the front door where she greeted Big Al with open arms.

"Come on! Annie's fast asleep in her bed." Glenda grabbed Alan's bigger than average hand and pulled him toward the kitchen. "I'm starving and would love a drink. Your father left his best bottle of Sullivan's Cove whisky out on the counter. He said it's divine. Have you had it before?"

"It's a family tradition. He gave me a bottle when I graduated," Alan grinned.

"Lucky you. And not just for the whisky, but *you* actually graduated. How does it feel?"

"Great, absolutely great to be away from that staunch campus. I thought I'd go crazy there."

"Oh, you poor baby. Four years at Princeton and you had it sooo bad." Glenda made a face and stuck her tongue out at Alan.

"Well, you could've finished school, well…if, well…"

"I know, if, if, if. My life is full of ifs." Glenda lifted her glass, "Here, let's toast to ifs."

"Hey there, slow down!" Alan patted Glenda on the back, after taking such a large swallow she began to choke. "You have to sip this stuff, girl. It's powerful. Maybe we should add some ice to yours."

"And cool me off? No thanks. I like the heat I feel when I'm around you, and the whisky makes me even hotter. Feel," she said, pulling his hand to her bare neck and guiding it slowly to her breast.

Alan sat his glass on the island and picked Glenda up with both hands clasped to her tiny waist. He placed her effortlessly on the countertop and began unbuttoning her blouse. She watched his big fingers clumsily paw at the small buttons and when he couldn't get the first one undone, she brushed his hands away and slid off the counter. "You never were good at that. Come on, I'm starving. Go start the pit outside, and let's put some good old-fashioned burgers on the grill."

"Aye, aye, Captain." Alan saluted and slapped her on the bottom as she bent over to remove items from the refrigerator. "Bring the bottle when you come outside, Glen."

Glenda leaned against the refrigerator door and watched Alan walk away. She had always loved his broad back and the way his thick red hair curled at the base of his neck. "Oh my," she sighed and took a sip of the whisky, letting it sit on her tongue long enough to taste the intensity of its flavor. 'Barley from Tasmania with its deep red basalt soil' her stepfather had proudly described it. She let it trickle down her throat, this time with due respect.

Alan slid open the large patio door and walked determinedly toward the gas grill. He raised the cover with one hand while steadying his drink in the other. A spider leapt from the grill and landed on his shirt. He let go of the handle and fell backwards trying to brush the insect away. Landing on the ground, the glass of whisky still intact, he watched the spider run under a potted plant. "I hate spiders," he growled and downed the rest of his drink in one ballsy gulp.

Pete opened his eyes and lay still, thinking he had been dreaming about spiders. He sat up and stretched his arms upward. Gathering his thoughts, he looked around and spotted a man sitting on the floor, his back toward him.

"I'd know that slab of meat anywhere. Hey there, Big Al," he said cheerfully.

Alan jerked and his eyebrows lifted high at seeing his friend. "Good Lord, look what the cat dragged in," he chortled, giving Pete a lopsided smile while he hoisted himself up. "What the hell are you doing here?"

Pete grabbed Alan's arm and steadied him. "I'm here to see my wife. Is she here?"

"Uh, yes, she's here." And just as if it was a planned introduction, Glenda came through the opened door with the bottle of whisky in one hand and a plate of hamburger patties in the other. Upon seeing her husband standing there next to Alan, she dropped the plate of meat, but held tightly to the Sullivan's Cove.

"Oh no, oh no," she mumbled, looking down at the patties now hidden underneath the platter on the floor. Pete rushed over to pick them up as Glenda stared down at the top of his head.

"That excited to see me?" he said, looking up at her surprised expression.

"Here, I'll take those." Alan took the platter from Pete's hands and offered him a napkin. "I'll be right back with some fresh ones and a glass for you, Pete. That's some darn good whisky she's holding in her hand. Notice she didn't drop it?" Alan walked away chuckling, as cool as a cucumber, but when he entered the house, he looked over his shoulder and caught the innocence in his best friend's smile as Pete longingly searched his wife's face for an explanation.

"Hi honey," Pete said shyly. "It's me, your husband."

"I know it's *you*. My goodness, I thought I was seeing a ghost. Why are you here?" Glenda brushed passed him and plopped down on a chair.

"Aren't you glad to see me?"

"Well, you didn't even call and let me know you were coming."

"I tried to call. You were always unavailable, so I got worried, or really, I felt like something was wrong. We haven't talked since you left. Why haven't you called me?"

"I've been busy," Glenda retorted and crossed her arms defiantly. "Nothing's wrong, I've just been busy."

The couple sat silently in their awkwardness until Alan strolled in with three glasses and filled them each. He handed them out and said, "I'd like to make a toast to our new guest. What a surprise to see you, old buddy."

From her chair, Glenda lifted her glass half-heartedly and took a swallow before Pete could clink her glass. He turned to Alan and said, "Cheers!"

After some small talk, Pete walked back to the café to get his truck and freshened up in the guest room, a separate wing far away from the central activity of the home. They regrouped outside on the patio where the men dominated the conversation sharing high school stories – their silly pranks, girls they dated, and teachers they either hated or tried to win over. Glenda sat back and watched them cautiously.

Curiosity weighed heavily on Pete, and he finally began

asking questions that he had set aside until everyone was comfortable. "Where's your mom and stepdad," he directed the question to Glenda.

"They, well, they're on a cruise."

"A cruise? While you're here all alone?" Pete frowned at the idea. Then he looked curiously over at Alan. "What brings you here? Don't you live somewhere in the city?"

"I do. I have a flat there. I just happened to be coming out here to see my dad. I didn't know they were traveling. Kind of surprised me that they would leave without taking Glenda."

"I didn't want to go," Glenda blurted. "I've never wanted to float around on a giant hotel. All you do is eat, drink, and sleep on those things. Not for me."

"I'm hungry," a child's voice spoke from the doorway.

"I bet you are." Alan quickly released his drink and lifted the little girl in his arms. "Annie, this is my best friend from high school. Say hello to Mr. Pete."

"Hi," Annie said and then shyly buried her face in Alan's neck. "I'm hungry, daddy."

Pete forced a smile and caught Alan's eyes. He silently mouthed with his head cocked, "Daddy?"

Alan rolled his eyes and turned to take Annie to the kitchen. "I'll be back. I've got to feed this growing girl." He peered over his shoulder at Glenda. "Maybe you can explain it all to Pete."

Glenda froze.

"When did Big Al get married?" Pete questioned.

"He's not married, Pete. But it's all amicable, and he's fathering his child, just as he should."

"Well, that's honorable. He looks like he's a good dad. Is he?"

"Oh yes, he is. He loves that little girl a great deal."

"But how did he raise her while going to college? Or did the mother raise her?"

"His father and well, my mother helped out. Annie's mother, well, she isn't in the picture very often. Let's don't talk about it. It all worked out fine."

Pete scratched his head. "Why didn't you tell me about this? I mean, every time you come to visit, don't you see the little girl?"

"I, I think if Alan wanted you to know, he would've told you. Let's respect that, shall we? Have another drink while I clean up the dishes."

It was true, Pete hadn't talked to Big Al in nearly a year, since the friend's wedding. He wondered why he didn't say anything then about having a child. He sat there thinking and hoping that the alcohol would soon mask his growing discomfort.

"Come on, let's go for a walk," Glenda coaxed while passing him, heading toward the woods.

"What about Big Al and his kid?"

"He took her to the park."

"Oh, that's nice. Wait up, I'm coming!"

"Great idea," Pete said, as they walked down the pebbled path. "This is gorgeous land. No wonder you like coming here. And that house, my gosh, how many rooms does it have?"

"Six or seven, if you don't count the library, the office and the basement."

"Nice," was the only word that came to mind. "I imagine you have your own room." Pete looked over at Glenda, and when she didn't respond, he took her hand. "You look tense. What's the matter?"

"It's just that, well, you should've called first. I mean, I could've prepared better for you, and you wouldn't had to experience that awkward moment seeing Alan and his child. And vice versa. It made him pretty upset, you know."

"Upset? I didn't notice him acting any differently?"

"Well, good heavens Pete!" Glenda let go of his hand and turned to face him. "He left, didn't he?"

"To take Annie to the park. What'd you mean? That was a made-up excuse to leave?"

"Yes, it was." Glenda turned to walk away. "You just should've called me first, or not come at all," she yelled without looking back.

Pete stood under the canopy of trees and watched his wife disappear into the woods. Everything felt foreign to him, even Glenda. He wanted to follow her, scoop her up in his arms and force her to talk. But he had tried that often the past few months and to no avail as Glenda's dark moods intensified. He thought about getting in his truck and driving back home right then and there. It might have been the right thing to do, but he couldn't tear himself away from the idea of sleeping next to her. Surely, she'll snap out of this mood and fall into step, he rationalized.

He returned to the guest quarters and spread out on the bed with Robert Ludlum's latest novel. As they always did when he read, the hours passed without him noticing, and before he knew it, the sun had gone down.

The house was dark and quiet when Pete walked through the halls to the main living area. He was drawn toward the only light emitting from the kitchen. When he entered the room, he saw Glenda sitting with her back turned. She was so busy writing that she didn't hear Pete's light footsteps.

"Hey babe, what are you doing?" he asked, standing directly behind her.

"Good Lord!" she yelled, turning abruptly, scowling up

at Pete. "Don't you ever give people warning? You scared the crap out of me!"

"I'm sorry. I just saw that you were...well, what are you writing?"

Glenda turned the tablet over and protected it with both hands. "Nothing important, really. Are you hungry?"

"Not yet. But we could go out to dinner. We could walk over to that little café across the road. It looks kind of cozy. What'd you think?"

"Pete, I'm not feeling all that well. I know it's early, but I'd like to go to bed soon."

"Glenda," Pete pleaded, sitting down next to her, "you have to tell me what's wrong. You're acting strange, and why are you so mad at me? It can't be because I showed up here."

"Let's go to bed. I'll sleep with you in the guest room. I'm really tired. Maybe we can talk tomorrow." Glenda took his hand and Pete followed her, as he knew he would to the end of his life.

Their lovemaking was methodical and ended quickly. Glenda rolled over on her side and whispered, "Goodnight. Tomorrow will be a better day."

"Especially if you make pancakes for breakfast," Pete said, snuggling up to spoon his wife. Comforted by resting his hand on her soft midriff, he was asleep in seconds.

Glenda stayed perfectly still fighting back tears, until the warm breath caressing the nape of her neck lulled her to sleep.

❧

The next morning, when Pete woke to an empty bed, he hastily dressed. Hearing clattering in the kitchen, he strolled barefoot down the long hall, casually peeking into different rooms. Glenda was busy stirring batter and gently dropping a spoonful onto a hot skillet. Pete smiled at the sight of his woman making him pancakes. "You're the best. I haven't had pancakes since you left."

"Well, today's your lucky day. Grab a cup of coffee and sit down."

"What are your plans for today?" Pete asked.

"I think maybe you're right. We do need to talk. How about after breakfast?"

"Sure. I'd like that."

Glenda set the table and piled the pancakes on a platter sitting next to scrambled eggs steaming on a plate. Pete's eyes grew wide with pleasure. Breakfast was his favorite meal of the day anywhere he could get it. They sat in silence, except when Pete let out a few contented sighs in between bites.

"Pete, when you're finished, please meet me upstairs on the loft. I have something to show you." Glenda got up from her chair and left the room.

Pete gobbled down the last three bites and swigged the rest of his coffee. Climbing two steps at a time, he reached the top landing where he found Glenda sitting on the floor with a photo album in her arms.

"Sit down," she said, patting the empty spot next to her. Pete obeyed.

"You asked about Annie. This is Annie when she was born." Glenda pointed. "This book contains photos of her through the stages of her life up until now."

She handed the album to Pete. "Cute baby," he commented, glancing at each page. Flipping through them he stopped and looked up at Glenda curiously. "Where's a picture of Annie's mother?"

Glenda leaned over and picked up a considerably smaller

album that she had left sitting on a table. She put her hand over Pete's and squeezed it. Their eyes met. Then she placed the smaller album on top of the large one and slowly opened it to the first page. Pete looked down and froze at what he saw.

"That's you," he said flatly. "*You* are Annie's mother?"

Glenda nodded and kept her eyes on his.

Pete shoved the album aside. Feeling the wind knocked out of him, he clumsily stood up. "How can that be you? I don't understand. When did you find time to have a baby being at school and all?"

Glenda remained silent.

Resignedly, he dropped his hands to his side, as he began to put together the sordid past of the woman sitting before him. "And Big Al is the father? Wow, you had a baby with Big Al. But you said you'd never have children." He could not control his rising voice. "Not even with me! Never! This is nuts!"

"Pete, I was pregnant when I went off to school and didn't know it. And then my mother married Alan's dad, and everything went crazy. I didn't want to quit school, neither did Alan and the whole idea of our parents being married to each other felt so weird. We were devastated. We were too young to have a child. It just happened so fast." Glenda closed her eyes and started crying.

Pete wanted to reach out for her, but he couldn't find it within himself to do so. "But, Glenda, you lied to me all this time. And what about Big Al? Are you two together playing mommy and daddy every time you come here? How could you see your child, the father of your child and the man you once loved...or still do, hell, what do I know, and then leave them to come back home to me?"

"You don't understand. At the time I didn't want to

raise the baby, but Alan did, so my mother and his father decided they would until he got out of college. I had to go home and take care of dad. Don't you see? And I've been a part of Annie's life every time I come here, but each time I come, it gets harder and harder. Now, I can't possibly leave her."

Pete walked over to the window and stared out across the vast lawn, the dolphin fountain, and beyond the sculptured hedges. Another question flashed before him. "Does Annie know that you're her mother?"

"Not yet," Glenda said sheepishly, looking down at the picture of herself and her daughter the day she was born. "I planned to tell her yesterday, but you arrived."

Pete raked his fingers through his hair and blew out a breath. He couldn't believe what he was hearing. "You said you can't leave her. Just what does that mean?"

"I can't leave her."

"You can't leave her *here*? You mean you want to take her home?" Pete felt a flush of hope at the idea.

"No, Alan has guardianship and won't let her go. Neither will his father."

"What does your mother say?"

"She wants her here, too. They've all been raising her, it's only right. I don't have any choice, Pete. I have to stay. I'm sorry. I didn't want it to be this way. I thought I was strong enough. I thought that Alan…"

"Alan, what? That he'd decide to love you again, and that you'd be one big happy mixed family? Where do *I* fit into this big scheme? Do I just drive into the sunset and pretend that I don't love you, that you didn't lie to me, that our marriage wasn't a farce?"

Glenda bowed her head, silenced by the truth.

"Where do I fit in?" his voice softened.

"You don't." Clutching the album to her chest, she rose to her feet and walked past Pete into Annie's room.

Ambivalent about whether to stay or leave, Pete walked around in circles until he could find the courage to face Glenda again. He stood in Annie's doorway and watched Glenda sobbing into a pillow, as she lay curled up on her daughter's bed. To his left he spotted a picture of Big Al and Annie on the dresser. Glancing around the room, he saw watercolors that Glenda had painted. They were scenes from Good Hollow, the river, the fields, and children playing. He remembered watching her paint them from the covered porch he built just for her, the sadness on her face growing intensely with each stroke. Now he knew why. She was right, he did not fit in.

"Forgive me, Pete."

Half-conscious, Pete disregarded Glenda's muffled plea and walked out of the house to his truck. He drove fast and deliberately toward home. His world was capsized, and it wasn't until he stopped to get gas that he realized he was barefoot and had left his shoes.

Nearly two agonizing months passed by, and Pete had not heard one single word from Glenda. During that time, he had packed her things and as he did, he noticed that the picture album of their small wedding was missing. He felt the need to call and ask her if she had it. After the fourth ring, Pete started to hang up until he heard a gruff voice on the other end.

"Hello," Pete said after he cleared his throat. "Mr. Smith, is that you?"

"Yes, who's calling?"

"It's me, Peter Pickett. Glenda's, uh, Glenda's…"

"I know who you are Pete. It's rather ironic that you should call right now."

"Why's that?" Pete asked.

"Glenda just took off in the car heading your direction. She and my son had quite an argument. Seems there are some differences that haven't been ironed out yet. Has Glenda said anything to you?"

"Sir, Glenda has not spoken to me in weeks."

"Well, I know you are aware of Annie's situation and all, but this latest beats everything."

"'What do you mean? What can possibly be any worse than learning that Glenda has a child by my own best friend? That she's leaving me. Please top that, Mr. Smith!" Pete's voice rose uncomfortably high and when he heard himself, he quickly lowered it. "I'm sorry sir. It's just a lot to take."

"I understand. I do. It's been hard on all of us. And now…"

"Now, what?"

"She'll tell you everything. I imagine she'll arrive in a couple of hours – she took the next flight out. Good luck to everyone."

Pete held the phone to his ear for the longest until the flat dial tone warned him that no one was at the other end. Baffled, he went to the refrigerator to grab a beer. Out on the front porch swing, he sat in silence wondering what he was going to say to his estranged wife.

If the lights from the car coming up the driveway had not shown on Pete's face, he would have slept through the night. He rose to his feet unsteadily, rubbed his eyes, and watched a taxi driver open the trunk of his cab.

Glenda got out and stood behind the car while the driver unloaded her luggage. She paid him, and Pete heard her say,

"Keep the change," before she stepped aside and peered in the dark at the house.

Pete sat perfectly still and watched her. He waited before he let her know his presence. "Need help with your luggage?"

"Yes, I do," Glenda answered and within minutes, Pete and Glenda were standing in the living room, both wondering which room the luggage should go in.

"Well, I suppose you came to bring me the divorce papers," Pete said.

"That was the plan. But something has happened that may change that, should you agree."

"What? Big Al won't take you back?" Pete said snidely.

Glenda turned away, lowering her chin to her chest with a humility that Pete had rarely witnessed in the woman he thought he knew so well. "He never has wanted me back, Pete. That's why I married you."

"That's the only reason you married me?"

"Well, truthfully, there were many times I thought so," she spoke softly to her clasped hands, "but you're really a great guy, and I knew you loved me. I figured I'd learn to love you as much, someday."

Pete wanted to ask her if this was the day she loved him, but he once again wanted her to say it without persuasion. He stayed quiet, waiting, watching Glenda as she turned her back. When the room became unbearably silent, the question floating heavily in the air, Pete felt his heart sinking fast. "Turn around, Glenda."

Glenda turned slowly.

"Why are you here?"

"I'm going to have your baby."

The next seven months went by as if nothing had happened. The baby in Glenda's belly grew as God had planned, and her visits to New York continued as usual. Each time she returned it took her several days to recover. The stories about Annie made her cry, but she kept them mostly to herself and went about busily preparing for their son's birth.

On the night of her final return from New York, as Glenda had ignored the doctor's orders not to fly in the third trimester, Pete waited on the porch swing for her arrival. Against his wishes, she had insisted that she take a cab, as it would be a late flight. Sitting in the dark remembering the last time he had waited for her, an uneasy feeling crept over him. He began to worry until a car finally pulled into the driveway. The unmistakable silhouette of a man in uniform appeared in front of the headlights.

"Mr. Pickett? Pete Pickett?" The officer approached, landing one foot firmly on the bottom step of the stairs.

"Yes sir," Pete answered and stood at attention.

"I am sorry to inform you that your wife is in the Trenton hospital and that you might want to get over there as soon as possible. I don't have any more information other than that, but if you'd like a ride…"

"What happened? Is she alright? Is she having the baby?" Pete steadied himself against the post.

"Sir, I don't know anything else, but that you should probably go now."

"I'm on my way. Thanks Officer, I'll drive myself."

The accident had happened just two miles from their home the doctor explained, and the taxi driver had died at the scene. Glenda was unconscious when they brought her in and that was considered a blessing, as the damage to her head and neck was severe. Although the baby was three weeks shy of full term, he had survived delivery. Glenda, however, remained heavily sedated for several days after, and when she awoke, Pete was by her side. He would never forget her last words asking for forgiveness and his own when he whispered, "I wanted so much to be the better man."

Pete had no idea how long he had sat in his truck in the hospital parking lot staring at the decaying banana. The last thing he remembered was that he had been instructed to notify the family that Glenda Anne Picket had died. He held the banana in his hand and squeezed it until the warm, mushy insides poured out between his fingers, and then the tears erupted.

The day arrived to take his child home from the hospital. Glenda's mother was there to hire a nanny and to try and convince him to let her raise the baby in New York. Pete was infuriated by the suggestion and insisted that she leave the next day.

Six months later, Pete left his attorney's office and went to visit Glenda's grave. He stood to the side of the headstone and placed a bouquet of flowers in front of it, trying not to think of the final days with his wife, but of the first year of marriage that he hoped would have been the beginning of a lifetime of wonderful. He told her that little Pete had held his spoon by himself that morning but refused to eat the creamed spinach – a stubborn streak he had surely inherited from his mother.

Always uncomfortable in a suit, he loosened the tie and laid down on the thick layer of scattered leaves next to the gravesite. Letting his body go limp, his eyes followed a jet's lingering contrails until they began to dissolve. What he had to say next would be easier while looking up at the heavenly blue sky.

"You might have been right when you told me that I took advantage of you at a weak period in your life. I'm sorry. I'm sorry for trying to force you to love me. I don't know what we were playing at. I thought, well, you know what I thought." He went on to tell her more, and he shared with her his respect for Big Al's desire to be a good father and raise Annie. But when he came to the part he had been saving for last, the words soured on his tongue. "I suppose I should thank you for wanting to give me a child...even though... even though he's Big Al's child and not mine. The red hair is a dead giveaway, Glenda. I wonder if you knew. I wonder."

He left the gravesite drained but determined to set things right. When he arrived at his home, the nanny was sitting on the front porch with little Pete fast asleep in her chubby arms. Pete smiled, caressed the child's thick, curly red hair, and went inside. He stood in front of the phone and said a little prayer before he picked up the receiver. "Lord, help me be the better man." A single tear trickled down his cheek.

When Big Al answered, Pete avoided the customary salutation and said, "Hey, it's your old pal, Pete. I know we haven't talked since the funeral, but how would Annie like to meet her brother?"

KISMET

It was their second marriage, and it happened fast. Not a shot-gun wedding, but just as awkward, yet convenient for both, as Anita and Cliff were not the kind of people who needed those long melodramatic wasted months to recover from a divorce, like so many others did. They desperately craved and depended on love to redefine themselves, ease the pain, and erase the past. In other words, they just could not bear the thought of being alone...so they married.

If her first husband had not traveled so much, leaving Anita with too much time to spare, she would not have sought out Cliff sitting on the Venice Boardwalk sulking over an ex-wife who had left him in a state of vulnerable shambles. His sad little face, those cute scarred up surfer knees, and that hopeless gaze into the ocean, was simply irresistible. But it was kismet that brought them together, she had convinced Cliff after she rolled past him on roller skates unnoticed, until finally on the fifth round, determined to get his attention, she faked a fall and strategically landed right in his lap. The collision jolted Cliff from his stupor and moved Anita into a perfect position to capture the miserable king, and so, she did.

A quick amicable divorce from the husband who finally confessed he was not actually traveling *just* for business and a courthouse wedding not much later to lonely Cliff, who had been miserably couch surfing and was quite eager to sleep in a nice bed – twin, double, California king, no matter – the couple started their new life together.

Shortly after, Anita inherited her grandfather's soybean farm south of Cleveland, Ohio. The newlyweds, seeking an affordable adventure outside of Los Angeles and Anita hoping to move them as far from Cliff's ex-wife as possible, decided that once again, kismet was offering them a second chance at a new life in the hearty and bountiful farmlands of the Midwest.

Still young and energetic in their early thirties, turbocharged libidos intact, and at a time during the seventies when caution was easily cast to the wind, the couple bid farewell to the cultural mecca, a paradise of idyllic weather where they had spent their entire lives and drove with wild abandon for thirty-four hours to their new home two-thousand miles away.

When they arrived, they stood speechless before the twenty-something acres of land sitting neatly off the main highway, a good distance from the Cleveland city limits. What an enormous change leaving L.A. where trees were replaced with buildings to the vast countryside where houses were traded for soybeans. Never had they experienced sweet smelling air, such intense quiet, and views without smog for miles and miles. Emotions were on high seeing their new home for the first time darkly hidden within a thick grove of humongous, foreboding trees. They silently agreed to adapt to this rather disturbing, but interesting new life and went about learning a daily routine fueled by rebounding love.

If only that had been enough.

The house turned out to be older than Anita's grandfather, and everything in it was outdated and in need of repair. Neither had any experience with homeownership, having lived in apartments their entire adult lives, the maintenance man living two floors below. They had barely enough cash to employ a handy man to at least repair the essentials, like a toilet that didn't flush. And, what's a soybean, anyway? Upon agreement, the neighboring farm would maintain their fields and keep most of the profit in exchange for keeping the old house pest free. A convenient arrangement, since they owned a company called *Assassin Vermin Control* and rats, moles and shrews were their specialty. "The last thing you want to experience is a face-to-face introduction with a diseased rodent!" That warning and the dried and stiff skins hung across the neighbor's fence cinched the deal.

Finding a good job would be necessary, and soon they learned, nearly impossible.

Neither openly admitted that they were secretly missing the warm sun that had been a constant halo back home and the beaches full of every walk of life. Nor did they share their fear of what winter might bring after the local grocery store owner sternly cautioned them that the farmer's almanac predicted a very cold winter ahead for Ohio. They were certain that he was just taking advantage of two naïve city slickers, but to be on the safe side, they purchased a week's supply of canned food, and upon the proprietor's insistence, they hired his nephews to cut enough wood that could start a bonfire tall enough to be seen all the way from Pennsylvania. They felt foolish, but, at least, prepared.

They soon found out that flip-flops had no use on the

rugged farm. Fortunately, the grandfather had left behind his winter clothing, long-johns and boots, hats, mufflers and gloves, and Anita sorted them out for both to wear after beating the dust from them while hanging on the outdoors clothesline. Feigning confidence that they were now ready for a rare experience, cold and snow, the first fire of the year was built in the vast fireplace that took up an entire wall where nearby, rocking chairs and piles of blankets sat waiting. The experience was unlike anything they had imagined, and soon they began to feel as old and decrepit as the house.

As the days grew nippier, Anita and Cliff grew more irritable, and after dinner one evening, while sitting in front of a roaring fire passing a bottle of whiskey between them, they could no longer contain their inner fears.

"Have we made a mistake?" Anita asked the loaded question while hypnotically staring into the leaping flames.

"Well, we asked for an adventure, and we got one." Cliff's blasé response could not be helped, and he wished he would have said something more enthusiastic, but even the whiskey wasn't enough to mask the truth.

"You don't sound very convincing, Clifford." And at that moment, she was surprised that she had called him by his full name, a name he hated.

And clearly, so was Cliff. "Oh really?" He stomped his foot on the floor, stopping the chair from rocking and turned to look at her, a serious scowl she had never seen before crossing his youthful brow. "You never call me Clifford unless you're mad at me."

Anita stared ahead at the flames now licking hard at the logs, as if her internal angst had somehow aggravated them.

"Don't be mad at *me*," he stated defensively. "You know, this wasn't *my* idea."

Anita stiffened. And neither was marrying me – the

dismal truth occurred to her. She dare not say that aloud. Silence was all she had to offer, and Cliff was emboldened by it.

"And please don't tell me it was kismet." He stood abruptly and thrust the bottle in her face. "Here, take this before I say something I'll regret. I'm going to bed. Goodnight!"

Sitting there in the rocking chair listening to her husband brush his teeth, turning off the water faucet each time the pipes rattled, she couldn't explain the uncomfortable feelings she'd been having since the first night they slept in the strange house. The walls, ceilings and even the floors built in drab colorless splintered wood felt like they were sucking the life out of her, and the small scratched and dull window-panes barely let any light enter to brighten her imagination. Worst of all, there was a lingering stench of someone's miserable deteriorating past coming from somewhere deep within the walls, that Cliff claimed he could only smell in their bedroom. Even their lovemaking had ceased, dimmed by the disenchantment of their decision and the unknown future, not to mention again, the foul smell in the walls.

Anita's happiness had always been her top priority, and Cliff was failing her in that department. She sensed him vacillating between wanting to make it work and wanting to run away. On an honest day, she admitted she did the same, but there was no place to run.

They went to bed defeated, without another word and slept back-to-back, eyes staring into the dark as the wind whistled through the cracks of the windowsills, hinting at an impending doom.

The next morning, Cliff, layered in t-shirts and wrapped in an old bomber jacket, left to get the mail, and later returned with news for Anita. "I got a letter from my cousin. Looks like my uncle is dying and wants to see me before he goes. It's possible he has left me an inheritance." Cliff's eyes lit up for the first time in a long while.

"Oh really? I didn't know he was wealthy," Anita said passively without considering the imminent death of his family member since her husband's sudden spark of interest in the inheritance obviously took precedence.

"Well, yes, I suppose he is. He lives in Malibu. It takes some money to live there, you know. But, more importantly, my uncle *is* dying. So, while I was in town, I booked a flight to L.A and am leaving tomorrow morning."

Anita now turned her full attention toward Cliff and let the skillet she was scrubbing slip back into the sudsy water. She wiped her hands on the stiff apron that came with the house and took a deep breath. "You bought only *one* ticket?"

"Well, yes, I didn't think we could splurge on two tickets in such a short notice. This one set us back nearly five hundred. And besides…" Cliff caught the hurt in Anita's eyes. Or was it fear? He couldn't afford to acknowledge either and continued to make his case. "I'll be back in a week or so, depending on my uncle's situation, and maybe with some good news for both of us."

Still feeling off kilter from the night before, Anita went back to scrubbing and let her thoughts wander to the beautiful beaches of California. They seemed a lifetime away.

The next morning, Cliff was gone.

As the days passed, the nights grew longer, and the skies filled with grey, thick nimbostratus clouds. Cliff called only once, and in a hurried conversation explained that he would be attending his uncle's funeral followed by a hearing of the will, and the dates were not yet determined. Anita slept restlessly, and soon dark rings appeared around her eyes. She so much hated being alone.

While she was in town one morning prospecting for a job, she sat in an ice crème parlor lethargically sipping on a root beer float and searching the want-ads. The tv was on overhead, and the program was interrupted by a weather report. A storm was on its way and predicted to land by dusk. Warnings were administered with severe tones followed by a long list of necessities in preparation for the excess of snow. Tensing up, Anita took leave of the cozy parlor and charged toward the hardware store where Zeb, the proprietor, also posing as the town's weatherman, would explain what was ahead. Fresh out of flashlights, he sold her every candle on the shelf and a double dose of fear.

Before she drove back to the house, she stopped at a convenience store with the only telephone booth for miles around. She felt the sudden urge to call her mother before the storm hit and possibly left her without phone service, as Zeb had warned. Besides, she needed to hear a familiar voice, even if it was her apprehensive, although loving mother.

"Mom, how are you?" she spoke into the heavy black phone piece, holding it far enough away from her mouth to avoid any germs from the previous caller.

"Oh, honey, I am fine. But how are *you*?" she asked in a worried tone; the one she had used when advising her against marrying again so quickly after divorce and moving to Ohio for the reasons Anita now understood.

"I'm good. This has really been an enlightening experience here. Even groovy," she winced when she heard herself say the word. Talking to her mother always brought the inner child out.

"Groovy? I'm surprised you feel that way. I thought you'd be really upset. Your dad and I were going to call you tonight to talk about it."

"Oh mom, please. I can handle a storm without Cliff here. I'm stocked up and ready to build my first snowman!" The fake chuckle didn't faze her mother.

"Honey, we're here for you. You know that. I mean, your first divorce happened so fast, we didn't have time to help you. And now, you're there all alone in a strange place without any support. I admire your strength, but are you *really* okay?"

Anita stood perfectly still, suddenly aware that she had been watching a rather large ominous-looking bug climbing up the side of the booth toward her and not really paying attention to what her mother had said. Then it sunk in. "Mom, you're not just talking about me being alone in a storm by myself, are you?"

A swallow stuck in her throat while waiting for her mother's reply.

"I'm talking about your divorce, Anita. I ran into Cliff's sister today at the mall, and she told me everything. I told you that you should've waited to marry him until he got over his first wife, and now…"

"What are you saying? What about his first wife? What are you saying?" Anita heard the upsurge in her voice; the words ricocheting off the dingy glass walls.

"Oh my, don't tell me you don't know. How could that be?"

"Good Lord, mom! Don't know *what?*"

93

"Cliff is divorcing you and going back to *her*."

Anita froze, dropped the phone, and smashed the bug with her purse.

"I can't believe you didn't know this. But honey, I did warn you, and by the way, the good news is you're in time to get a simple annulment. Sounds much better than divorce, don't you think? Anita, Anita, are you there?" her mother's words sounded far away from the receiver dangling on its cord.

Anita wasn't sure how she had driven home and missed seeing the first snowflake of the year hit her windshield. She didn't even feel the wind whipping around her leggings as she slowly walked from the makeshift carport to the front door of her grandfather's house. In her obliviousness, she stood long enough at the door to see a set of eyes peering back at her from the other side of the small paned window.

"Oh, you're back!" she exclaimed and quickly unlocked the door to greet Cliff. Only he wasn't there. In the stillness of the living room, only the wind blew wildly through the house searching for something to disturb.

"Oh, so, now I'm seeing things! Great! A delusional woman all alone in this creepy old house with a snowstorm on its way and miles from her cheating husband! Just great! Where's kismet now that I need it? What possible reason is there for me being stuck here?" She yelled at the top of her lungs, "Is anyone listening?"

Feeling unglued, Anita was startled out of her fit when the front door banged hard against the wall, and before she could reach it, it closed by itself. "Oh, I need a drink!"

After warming her body and numbing her mind with whiskey, Anita went outside and carried loads of firewood into the house. She placed all thirty-nine candles by the big box of kitchen matches on the coffee table. She filled the deep claw-footed bathtub, the sink and several buckets with water and poured ice into a cooler where milk, beer, butter, and her favorite yogurt could last for a few days.

Secure that she was set for the storm, her thoughts of Cliff returned. "How could he leave me all alone like this?" Bundled up on the sofa, the fire warming the house, she finished off the bottle of whiskey and cried herself to sleep. As she slept, the snow fell, and fell, and fell.

Dreams came rarely in Anita's sleep, but on this cold wintry night, outside everything blanketed in snow, she had a strange and haunting dream. She saw her face in front of a flame of fire as if she were searching, a torch guiding the way. Snow flurries danced around her naked body, so thick she could not see past them, yet she felt an allover warmth on her glowing skin as she moved through the cold air. From behind, strong arms wrapped around her, unfamiliar, but unmistakably a man's arms. His soothing touch nearly brought her to her knees. She searched for his face, finding nothing but snow.

"Who are you?" she asked. "Please tell me who you are."

First, arms slowly appeared, then a neck and just when a pair of smiling lips landed on hers, something loud and disturbing woke her from the dream and the scene vaporized.

The last log in the fireplace had dropped and was quickly being consumed by the embers. At the same time, unbeknownst to Anita, a tree limb had cracked from the weight of the snow and fallen on the carport and severed the overhead electric wire to the house.

Clearing her head, Anita sat up and looked around. She was certain that she had left the light on in the kitchen and a nightlight by the front door. Reaching for the candles, she lit several and brought some life back to the dark and eerie room. Unbundling her body from the blankets, she felt a cool air slap at her wet skin. She had been sweating, and the room was now cold and without artificial heat or light. Then she remembered the dream and the tantalizing kiss and in the soft glimmer of light she felt a faint smile.

The kindling caught fire quickly and soon a new pile of dry logs was aflame. Outside dawn had greeted the storm and the wind howled like hungry wolves. Anita slipped on a second pair of her grandfather's thick wool socks and placed a cap over her dampened hair. One more time she picked up the house phone only to find no dial tone. She rummaged through the crammed closet of skimpy sundresses that now smelled like mothballs and wore one over her sweater. She put on her roller skates and imagined herself skating freely on the Santa Monica Pier. Reading by candlelight in front of the fireplace was nearly impossible. Anita had never felt so ancient and so very alone. Images of Cliff and his ex-wife together churning in her head only made matters worse. If only she had learned to knit.

Back under the blankets with eyes tightly closed, she tried to resurrect the dream, the flame, the snow and the man's lips, but decided it was best to keep her clothes on until he was identified. When she could no longer feel her tongue, she slipped into a deep dream state. There she was, riding on a Ferris wheel, high above the ocean. The wind was blowing fiercely, and the sun was hidden behind the clouds, but the ocean below was a calm, still blue. From behind she felt fingers slowly moving under her tucked armpits. "Oh my," she exclaimed, voluntarily lifting her arms to welcome his touch. And just when she did, the fingers began to tickle her, a soft tickle that made her giggle, and then a rough tickle, the kind her brother used to do and cause her to laugh so hard she would wet herself.

"Stop, stop!" she yelled, screaming in between the wheezing gasps, squeezing her arms against his hands. She felt her body fall to the floor and when she opened her eyes, she was just inches from the fireplace, and the hands were still tickling her. "Stop, stop!" she demanded again, and when she tried to push the hands away, she felt them alive in her grasp. Hands, real hands. Hands with skin and nails. And hair?

Anita sat up in horror, looked around the candlelit room and cried, "Who's there?" A cold chill took her by surprise and then she saw him. When she tried to stand, her legs collapsed beneath her. The figure moved toward her and caught her fall. Anita looked up and there before her was a man, or a teenager, or a combination of the two, confusing in the firelight. She jerked from his hold and crawled to the sofa. When she looked back, the man had sat down on the rocking chair, and with folded arms, stared at her with his large, round eyes, and a grin that would have stretched wider if there were more cheeks to help spread it.

"Who are you, and how did you get in?" her eyes darted over to the locked door.

Through the candlelight, she noticed that his hair was bright red and standing straight up, like Troll Doll hair, its tips pointing in all directions. He had on a green outfit, much like an elf's, with polka-dotted suspenders over a button-downed shirt. "Who are you?" she asked sternly, as if she were talking to a child.

"Whoever you want me to be?" he said, his eyes still so wide, the white encircled them. "I'm not here to hurt you, so you can get that out of your head right now," his voice starting out with a deep bass and ending in an adolescent whine. "Did you like the tickling?"

Anita pinched herself and tugged hard at her hair. "I'm

dreaming, I'm still dreaming," she declared, shaking her head loose, waving her hands wildly in the air.

"Don't think so," the man sang. "I am here and here to stay, and even your dreams can't make me go away."

"This is not happening. I'm hallucinating and need another drink, and some sleep, and for this storm to end!" She reached over for the bottle and drank it like a man about to face a leg amputation with an axe. When she had enough, she crawled back under the layers of blankets and closed her eyes, refusing to look at the rocking chair where a figment of her distressed imagination sat smiling.

The next morning, or perhaps it wasn't morning – she could not tell, because nothing had changed, the wind still blowing like mad, the house dark within, the candles burned out, save one. Squinting to read the hands on her watch, she was startled that she had slept twelve hours and it was now early evening. Remembering the dream, she looked over at the rocking chair where the man had tormented her, and nothing was there. Relieved, she went straight to the door and checked its lock. Still intact, she unlocked it and cracked it open to the roaring wind beating against the house. At least two feet of snow was piled up at the door. Anita slammed the door shut with the strength of her back.

"It's not over! How long can a storm last up here?" She rubbed her face in anguish and blew out a frustrated breath. "I'm hungry!"

More logs piled high, candles lit, and in her grandfather's boots, Anita went to the kitchen. Standing before the stack of canned vegetables, her thoughts turned to peanut butter and within seconds she had a peanut butter and jelly sandwich in hand.

"Eww, I hate peanut butter. How does it taste? Like dried

vomit mixed with rancid canola oil?" That nasally voice from the night before was back and this time in her kitchen.

Anita dropped the sandwich and jerked her head toward the voice. There he was, the figment, the dream, oh take that back, the nightmare, still in green, only now she could see his feet, and later she would wish she hadn't. Fear should have been her next reaction, but it didn't come. In the faint candlelit room, the man before her looked almost childlike.

"Are you a ghost?" she asked.

"Hmm, I don't think so. Ghosts don't have choices."

"Look, I don't want to be rude, but you *are* trespassing."

"Me? You invited me, toots. Don't you remember?"

Anita moved closer and stepped on the sandwich. "Oh, darn," she complained, lifting the boot, now smeared with peanut butter and jelly.

"Ha, ha, ha, ha, ha, ha," the spirit's voice rattled on like a machine gun.

Anita gave him a stern look, wiped the boot on the rug and looked up angrily. "So, if you're not a ghost, what are you?"

"Kismet."

"Kismet?"

"Yeah, Kismet. Kismet, Kismet, Kismet!"

"OK fine, we'll call you Kismet. Meanwhile, why don't you go pester someone else? I have enough on my mind."

"Like what? Like a weak, two-timing husband that abandoned you for sunny California just days before a major storm dumped three feet of snow on Cleveland?" He batted his hairless eyelids and one side of his wide grin dropped, creating a funny kind of sinister look that didn't match his clown-like half-moon shaped eyebrows.

"How did you know that?"

"I know a lot. So, what are you going to do about it, now that you're stuck here?"

"None of your business. Now go away, or I'll make another peanut butter and jelly sandwich and eat it slowly, right in front of you."

"Just try," the spirit teased, grabbing the jar and throwing it like a football into the fireplace.

The fire gobbled the container in a flash and spit peanut butter all over the hearth. "Eww, didn't mean to do that. Now we'll smell the vomit for days!"

"Look Kismet, or whatever your name is, I don't need any unwanted guests, spirits, or ghosts to keep me company. Now, please go away."

"I can't. You called for me, and I'm here to help you with your destiny. Until then, I got dibs on the sofa this time!"

Anita rushed past the man, now sprawled out on the sofa, his thin, hairy feet propped up on the arm. She slipped into a coat, grabbed her purse, and opened the window to crawl out. Halfway out, as far as she could see, everything was covered in white, even the tree limb that had fallen on the carport and imprisoned her car. The wind blew snow up her nose and into her eyes, and realizing there was nowhere to go, she inched back into the room and quickly shut the window.

"This is terrible, just terrible! I'm stuck here!" Turning to face the unwanted visitor, she saw that he had fallen asleep. With his eyes closed and his mouth shut, he looked harmless, almost angelic. She slowly walked toward him and stood just inches from his face. *Is he real? Or am I hallucinating?* Compelled to see for herself, she touched his nose. *Feels real.* When she leaned down to hear his breathing, the sleeping man kissed her on the cheek. Anita jerked back and felt her face. "Eww, wet lips. You *are* real!"

"Did you like it?" Kismet sat up and smiled.

"Not necessarily," she stepped back hesitantly, wondering why she hadn't just said a clear No! *Am I that lonely?*

"Well, *you* certainly can't go out there either, so until this storm passes, we might as well make the best of this." She tried not to look at his feet again. "Real or not, are you hungry?"

"No thanks, I don't eat. Gives me gas, and you definitely don't want that to happen in such close quarters."

"No, no, you're right, I don't, uh, well if you don't mind, I need to eat, so let me make another pea...well, a ham sandwich, and I'll join you in here."

"Lovely, I'll be right here, going nowhere, saying nothing, just waiting, looking as fetching as ever." He crossed his legs at the ankles, stretched further out, raised up on one elbow and put the other arm between his legs, covering the vital part. "The Burt Reynolds pose!" he declared, "Like it?"

Anita couldn't help but laugh at that one. Still, as she prepared her meal, she looked constantly over her shoulder to keep an eye on the strange man. He maintained his pose and his big eyes never let her out of sight and it was quite unnerving.

Well, he could've killed me in my sleep, so that's a relief. And if he was the man with his arms around me, that was pleasant, at least until he tickled the crap out of me. Hmmm.

Seated in the rocking chair across from her unwanted guest, she ate slowly while he watched. When she finished, she leaned back, closed her eyes and rested her head. She thought for sure when she opened them, he'd be gone.

No such luck.

After a while, she thought to ask, "So, Kismet, what did you mean you want to help me with my destiny?"

"First of all, let's cut to the chase. You have been abusing my name for years. Every important decision you've ever made, you made in the name of Kismet. Nothing you have ever done was because of fate. You planned, schemed, and decided on your own accord everything you did. Let's get that straight right now."

"OK, so what?" she looked at him quite annoyed.

"So, what? So, what? So, what?" Kismet jumped up and down on the sofa. "Do you hear yourself? So, what?"

Anita frowned, "What am I missing here?"

"I happen to know that you cheated in college, you sabotaged a co-worker to get her job, you trapped your first husband into marrying you, you manipulated Cliff while he was at his weakest, you moved here to run from his ex-wife that he loved with all his heart, and where has all this gotten you?"

"In a snowstorm in an ugly house all alone with you?"

"Yep, you said it sister! And everything you did you called it kismet. Would you like to take that back now?"

"Will it make you go away, if I do?" She ducked as if he would throw something at her.

"Only if you truly mean it, and only then," his smile widened as he picked up a candle and bit into it.

"Hey, hey, don't do that! I need those!"

"Do you mean it? Will you take it back and even apologize for using my name foolishly?"

"You're serious, aren't you?"

"Dead serious!" He chomped another piece off the end of the candle.

"OK, OK. Look, I didn't mean to use your name like that. I thought it was just a figure of speech."

"Wait, just a second. A figure of speech? To manipulate people and say, it's how fate would have it, just so you could get your way?"

"I, I…" Anita choked on her words.

"Think about it and talk to me in the morning. I'm tired. Nighty night!" And just like that, he was asleep, this time with a very loud and obnoxious sounding snore.

Cold in the bedroom without heat from the fireplace and alone with the wind and the dreaded snoring, Anita lay awake deep under the covers, thinking. She decided that even if she had lost her mind, and even if the strange being asleep on her sofa was a figment of her imagination, the things that he said were true. She let her mind drift back to her college days, her first marriage, and everything that had led up to now. It wasn't kismet, she had always known that. She would never allow herself to be duped by such an idea: something significant happening entirely by chance. *Ha! I would never have made it this far in life if I had. This far. This far? And look where this far got me.* And like being hit with a paintball upside the head, Anita realized that her life was nothing but a fake. Once again, she cried herself to sleep.

On the third day of the storm, the snow was still falling, and at this rate would soon reach a record three feet high. Groggy from a horrible night's sleep, she opened her eyes to a numb nose, and tears nearly frozen on her cheeks. She rushed into the living room to rekindle the fire. Kismet was nowhere to be found until she opened the pantry door, and he jumped out with a loud "Boo!"

"You almost gave me a heart attack!" she cried, forcing herself to sit down at the kitchen table.

He sashayed out of the pantry, gliding across the kitchen floor, his feet stuffed into cereal boxes. "What'd you think? Stylish, eh?"

"Hey, where's the cereal?"

He lifted the winter cap on his head and cereal fell from it, raining down on his shoulders like snow. Then he shook his head like a wet dog and the grains flew across the table, spraying into Anita's face, and one by one his smashed, red-tipped hair sprang back into place. Boing! Boing! Boing! Boing!

"You're nuts, completely nuts! I need that food," she cursed under her breath and insisted that he clean up the mess.

Refusing to do so, he sat down on the floor defiantly, "Now, tell me what you learned about yourself last night. And be honest!"

"Humph!" Anita swept some of the cereal from the table to a bowl and filled it with milk. "When was the last time you washed your hair?"

"Wash my hair and ruin this do? Quit changing the subject and let's get back to your confession."

"Well, I cried myself to sleep. What little sleep I had. But I cried because you're probably right. My life has been nothing but one manipulation after another, and…"

"And?" Kismet drummed his fingers on the wooden chair seat, faster and faster, "and, drumroll…"

"And…I'm sorry. I used kismet as an excuse for all my wrong choices. I know that now," and as if it had been directed, she began to cry.

Kismet stood and shuffled toward her, the cereal boxes crunching the flakes on the floor. Reaching out, he pulled Anita into his arms and held her. "You must allow yourself to trust fate," he said softly in a soothing, masculine voice. Through the blinding tears, she felt his strong embrace and for one glorious moment, she let it all go. She felt the man in her dreams holding her, caressing her arms and soothing her like no other had ever before. When she finally opened her eyes, Kismet was gone. Only the cereal boxes remained at her feet.

"I'm sorry," she whispered.

The day went by so very slow, Anita thought she would pull her hair out. In a strange way, she wished the weird figment of her imagination had stayed, at least through the storm. Alone with her newfound thoughts was unbearable. In a moment of sheer desperation, she picked up the phone and pretended to talk to a live person at the other end. She held the conversation for a good five minutes. She read the same books until her eyes crossed in the dull candlelight. Sleep was all she could depend on, and the dreams that came with it. But on this night, there would be very little sleep and no dreams.

A gentle light brought Anita to her senses after a long and restless night of delirium. Half awake, she crept to the window and saw that the wind had settled down and every-thing was still and white. The sun, barely peeking through the clouds and trees, shed a soft glow, promising better days ahead. It was so serene and beautiful, she thought she had died. Her eyes scanned the scenery and stopped at a shovel leaning against the house. That's it! She would shovel the three feet of snow to get to the car, but that didn't make sense; the fallen tree would keep her from getting to it. She needed help and all she knew to do next was to yell for it. So, that's what she did. She opened the window and yelled with all her might. Every hour on the hour until dusk fell, she yelled for help. When sleep finally came, she slept restlessly with a sore throat.

Day five since the storm began, and nothing had changed. The water too cold to bathe in, the firewood down to the last three logs, sick of canned vegetables and sandwiches, Anita began accepting her doom. How could she get out of the house with snow that deep? Could she wade through it to the neighbor's home twenty-something acres over? Were they even home? Why wasn't the electricity back on? Everything was still calm outside, no snow, no wind, no sign of life anywhere.

"I'm going to die here," and just when she said it, a crashing sound came from behind her. One of the skis that had been hanging on the wall had fallen to the floor. Looking down at it, she had a brilliant idea. She took the poles and the other ski down and threw them out the window. Settling on the ledge, she put the skis on, grabbed the poles and tried to stand. Then she heard it. A motor running from down the highway, the sound getting louder and louder as it came her direction. Determined, she took her first step forward, then her second, and within minutes she had moved ten yards from the house. Then thinking she had it made, she pushed herself forward and landed flat on her face. Trying desperately to get up, she kept falling into the snow that was now beginning to melt and slipped over and over again until too exhausted, she laid on her back and yelled to the heavens, "I'm going to die here, frozen to death! Is this my fate? Kismet, Kismet, where are you?"

The motor grew louder and louder as it approached Anita's home and then faded to nothing. Anita felt herself sinking into the snow and all was quiet in the slumberous stillness. Before she knew it, those wonderful hands that she had felt in her dreams picked her up and sat her inside a box, which was actually the cab of a big snowplow, where the warmth lulled her into a deeper slumber.

The next time she opened her eyes, she was tucked in her bed, the house was toasty, and the room was lit with a single candle. She had slept till after dark. She heard movement in the kitchen. *Oh, my goodness, he's back.*

Anita wrapped in a blanket, silently crept toward the figure. A man stood over the counter, his back toward her. Wrapping her arms around him from behind, she cried, "I'm so glad you're back. I've been so lonely."

The man slowly turned and placed his hands on her shoulders. When Anita looked up at the stranger, she cried, "Oh my God, who are you?" Stepping back, she slipped on the edge of the blanket, crumpled to the floor and hit her head. Everything in the room began to spin and within seconds, all turned to a shattered black.

Later, Anita awoke from a most wonderful sleep to find her face pressed against a firm chest of someone with strong arms steadily holding her body in place, her feet dangling as she was being held in a lap like a child. "Umm," she moaned, as a hand caressed her back. Thinking the dream had returned, she kept her eyes closed and immersed herself in it. "You feel wonderful. Please kiss me before I wake up," she said, letting her head fall back, her lips pursed and ready.

She felt her body being lifted higher, a hand gliding up her back toward her neck, and then a warm breath surrounding her mouth, followed by lips that met hers in the sweetest tenderness. As their mouths moved, she allowed the kiss to consume her and at that moment, she never wanted to open her eyes again. Never!

But, as all good things must come to an end, the kissing stopped, and Anita was forced to wake from the dream. She slowly opened one eye, holding the other tightly closed. Although it was a pleasant one, she didn't recognize the face smiling down at her, and when she forced the other eye open, instead of screaming, like she thought she would, or should, or maybe didn't have the energy to, she asked the man a most peculiar question, "Who sent you?"

"Kismet, I think," he answered.

Anita, desperate or delirious, it mattered not, reached around his neck and pulled him back to her eager lips, letting fate have his way.

RAINING PEPPERONI

*S*heila woke up feeling a little off. She had been having bothersome dreams, and this last one really nagged at her. It all started shortly after she read a story about a woman with a fetish for Paul Bunyan, the giant lumberjack in American folklore.

The first to arrive at work, she sat in her office in the stillness of the empty third floor, mulling over the dreams. Outside her window she could see the sun creeping up behind the downtown buildings. That majestic setting would usually trigger a prayer to start her day, but the dreams were predominantly all she could think about.

She imagined her desk wiped clean: gone was the cardholder with the tiny Greek gods lined up in a row, the tall coffee cup with a woman warrior etched in its side that held her pens and pencils, a pair of stylish readers, scissors, and the gleaming gold letter opener. The tissue in the trash can, tiny flower-scented notes, a hand-painted coaster from her niece, and the picture of her dog, Ziggy, she visualized them all stuffed in a coffin; the lid matching the top of her cherry-wood desk. Just as it was in the first dream.

As the nostalgia set in, she reflected on her career: eleven years sitting at this very same desk editing stories for a women's magazine with a team of women she admired and enjoyed. Hard to believe that nine females working in such close quarters on the same floor, in the same building for that long would not, by now, have shed some blood. It was almost like a sisterhood in a convent, only these women enjoyed showing off their newest outfits, celebrating birthdays, and cuddle days for someone hurting, and sometimes giving a free make-over to whoever needed a boost, followed by drinks at Lucy's Bar. It was like *The Golden Girls* times three, a good life, a wonderful career and all based on beautiful, artful lies – fiction.

Then why the dreams and the feeling of dread? Her thoughts were interrupted by a grinning co-worker sticking her head through the door and holding up a plump glazed donut. Sheila was thankful for the diversion, and her weakness for pastries led her straight to the kitchen.

A busy morning kept her rambling thoughts subdued until while at lunch, she leaned over and said to her friend and fellow editor, "Bernice, I've been having the strangest dreams. Can I share this last one with you?"

"Of course." Bernice, forever dieting and picking pepperonis off a slice of pizza, moved in closer, all ears. A widow at sixty, Bernice was the last of the original employees and had packed in forty years with the magazine. She was Sheila's mentor from the start, and they were like mother and daughter, trusting each other implicitly.

"OK, don't freak out, because you and others here are in the dream. I mean, let's not jump to conclusions." Sheila waited to get Bernice's usual expression, one eyebrow lifting the entire left side of her face – proof that she was actually listening and not just editing her words as she was so highly trained to do.

"Of course," Bernice repeated.

"Well, a bunch of us, and some faceless people, that happens a lot in my dreams, were eating pizza in the presentation room. Nothing unordinary, but the pizza boxes were stacked to the ceiling in the middle of the room, and we had looks on our faces like we were all going to explode as we stuffed our mouths full. Overhead was a giant size axe, you know, like the one Paul Bunyan carried, but as big as a sectional sofa. It was swinging freely in the air, and in between bites we kept looking at it like we were afraid of it."

Sheila took a moment to clear her throat and consider the next words. "Then...the strangest thing happened. You started a pizza fight and smashed a piece of pepperoni pizza in a co-worker's face."

"I did?" Bernice grinned, as if she were checking that off her bucket list. "Let me guess, was it, Alisha's face? She's been getting on my nerves lately talking about that new husband and a little too descriptive of their sexual escapades. Honestly, I..."

"Bernice!" Sheila scolded. "May I finish the story, please?"

"Of course."

Bernice's favored response made Sheila stop and count how many times she had said 'of course' since the conversation began. *Three!* The curse of editorship would forever plague them both.

"Well, so everyone's throwing pizza, and I'm yelling something at them but they're not listening. Now mind you, if it had been creme pies, I would have been the champion thrower. But pizza? So, no one is listening to me, and hundreds of tiny round pepperonis start falling from the ceiling like rain, and I try to escape but I'm trapped, and then suddenly this woman, a woman I've never seen in real life or even in a dream, starts climbing up the pizza boxes. That big guy, Paul Bunyan is standing at the top with his hands on his hips. She pushes him off and jumps on the axe, swoops down and begins chopping off our heads."

"WHAT?" Bernice's jerk sent the slice of pizza she had been holding, up in the air and face-down on the table. "That's terrible!" She looked as if she'd just watched Sheila spit in her plate. Then her eyes grew wide as curiosity took its hold. "Did my head get chopped off, too? I mean, what did *that* look like?"

"Oh Bernice, honestly! Do you think I stayed asleep long enough to see *that*? I woke myself up. Wouldn't you?"

"Of course." Bernice pondered the question, having answered too quickly, as Sheila shuddered, unable to stop herself from counting. *Four!*

"But actually…it really depends on whose head got chopped." Bernice's sinister grin made Sheila chuckle. "And raining pepperoni? Wow, cool dream…well, before the axe murderer, I mean. Who do you think she was?"

Elbows on the table, chin resting on her knuckles, Sheila contemplated the question. "I've thought and thought about that, but I don't know. It's been really bugging me."

'What did she look like?"

"Anyone, everyone really, except she had a large black mole on her chin, or else that was a pepperoni," Sheila sighed. "Thing is, I had similar dreams three nights this week. One, where all my office things were dumped in a coffin. Don't you think that's important? I mean, I'm not good with signs, but this one is screaming for attention."

"Coffin? Just what are you eating before you go to bed?"

Sheila shrugged her shoulders and let out another exasperated sigh.

"Look," Bernice, having lost interest in her lunch, shoved the plate of pizza to the side, "I've got a deadline to meet. Let me do some research about pizza, axes, rain, and moles in dreams. Oh, by the way, what was I wearing in the dream?"

"Good heavens, Bernice. I didn't notice *that.*" Sheila got up, shoved her chair under the table and took her uneaten salad to her desk. She had deliberately left out the part that all the ladies were naked, and everyone looked the same, like a Pillsbury doughboy with a huge butt. But who in their right mind would tell a chronic dieter, like Bernice, that?

"Meet me after work at Lucy's?" Sheila yelled at Bernice, stretching her neck out from inside her office.

"Of course," Bernice grinned.

Pleased with her day's work, despite the nagging sensation that something was brewing caused mostly by the dreams, but also having noticed that Mildred, the Editor-in-Chief was avoiding them, Sheila left the building in a hurry toward Lucy's bar, a short walk away. She arrived just minutes before Bernice.

"So," Bernice blurted, plopping down her purse on the stool next to Sheila, "I couldn't find anything on pizza or moles in dreams, but the being-trapped-thing means a change is needed. The axe killer, well, that's probably just Lizzy Borden resurrected. So, are you wanting a change in your life?"

"Not any more than usual. I like my job, my apartment,

my car...and yeah, I could use a good man and maybe a new hairstyle. What else is there?"

"Of course! That's it! You're going to meet a lumberjack who owns a vegetarian pizza restaurant called "Axe the Meat." Picture this: his biz sign will have a giant axe hovering over a bunch of women riding on the backs of cows with, like, broccoli wreaths in their hair, carrot whips in their hands, lettuce skirts, green bean anklets...wow, I could go on and on with this!"

"Right, and rabbit fur shoes, showing the hypocrisy of it all. Don't eat the rabbit, wear it instead." Sheila leaned back, much too serious, taking the fun out of Bernice's inter- pretation.

"Well, I was thinking more like carved out sweet pota- toes," Bernice frowned. "So, how about the lumberjack idea?"

"A lumberjack, hmm, I would consider that. Although, I'm not a big fan of plaid." Sheila just knew there was more to the dreams than that.

The two friends eventually parted ways after agreeing that they should at least talk to Mildred, just in case some- thing unusual was transpiring. On her way to her car, Sheila thought about the last thing Bernice had said, "Rain in a dream suggests sadness, and coffins can mean a new begin- ning." She had ignored the comment earlier, but in fact, there was a small dark cloud hanging over her head that she couldn't explain, and as for a new beginning, maybe that was about Bernice's retirement. Maybe she was realizing how much she was going to miss her favorite colleague. Maybe, maybe, maybe. The word was beginning to annoy her.

She stood on the sidewalk looking dreamily up at her company's mid-century office building. The moon was directly overhead spreading a warmth of light across its brick façade. In all these years she had never seen it in this kind of magical light. Across the way she saw one of Austin's popular moonlight towers, standing an impressive 165 feet in the air since they were first erected in 1895. From there she spotted the glow from the ring-beam exterior structure of the Long Center for Performing Arts. Many times, she had sat on that lush hillside people watching while sipping white wine disguised in a thermos. She loved her city, and for some reason, now more than ever.

Her eyes trailed back to her building where she noticed the light was on in Mildred's office. Impulsively, she went back inside and took a moment just to look around. With so few people there after hours, she was able to see things she would normally miss on those hectic days scrambling to meet deadlines; like that star engraved in the tile, and a wheelchair sitting off to the side. How long had those things been there?

She took the stairs to the third floor, as she sometimes did to clear her head. All office lights were off, except for the one coming from under the Editor-in-Chief's door. As she walked toward it, she heard voices, their words overlapping, as if in an argument. She stopped to listen. The door opened slightly, so she moved quickly down the hall and out of sight. Rounding the corner, the voices grew louder as the conversation continued outside Mildred's office door.

"Get a grip Mildred! It's going to happen, whether you like it or not. If anyone gets wind of this, I'll know it was you. I warn you now, the owner will be very unhappy if it does. Capiche?"

"I know when I'm beaten, Ms. Bunson. You've made yourself loud and clear!" Mildred retaliated and slammed the door behind her.

Sheila peeked around the corner and saw the elevator doors close. She contemplated knocking on Mildred's door but decided not to when she heard her crying and babbling to herself. As she entered the elevator, Mildred yelled from her doorway, "I quit! I quit now! Do you hear me, Ms. Bunson?"

Quit? Mildred is quitting? What's going on here?

When Sheila landed in the lobby, she thought about going back upstairs to talk to Mildred. But when she spotted the woman that she thought might be Ms. Bunson, she hid behind a tall plastic plant and suspiciously watched the woman leave the building and walk determinedly down the sidewalk. Sheila quickly followed. To her surprise, the woman walked straight into Lucy's Bar.

The bartender, having seen Sheila earlier, acknowledged her with his eyes and was about to say something until Sheila put her finger to her lips to hush him and slipped into a dark booth. As an aspiring detective, he winked at her and turned to tend to the new arrival. After he handed the woman a martini, he casually walked over to Sheila's booth.

"What gives?" he whispered, pretending to wipe the already clean table.

"I'm not sure yet, Vince, but I think that woman is trouble for my company. Can you keep her busy? Maybe find out her name?"

"Sure, Sheila. Whatever you say. This sounds like fun. It's been a boring day so far." Vince was so enthused, he nearly skipped back to the bar.

The woman opened her briefcase and removed some papers. With head bent, she read them while sipping on her drink. Sheila claimed the seat next to her.

Vince walked up, biting away a wicked smile. "Ms. Bunson," he said loud and clear, "can I get you anything else?"

"No," she said flatly without looking up.

His lip curled in disdain but morphed into a smile when he looked at Sheila who was evidently satisfied when hearing the woman's name. He knew then he had served her well and was eager to get into the game. "First time here?" he asked Sheila.

"Well, yes," Sheila played along, looking around the room as if she'd never seen it before. "Cute place. Who's Lucy?"

"Oh, Lucy? She's the owner's girlfriend. I'd introduce you but she's dead. Poor thing. This used to be a house of ill repute, and Lucy was...shall I say, the main dish." Vince offered a sly wink. "But *I'm* here now to serve you. What would you like?"

Hambone, Sheila thought just as Ms. Bunson looked over at her with an air of disapproval. Sheila's eyes landed directly on the black mole near her chin. She could barely stop the surprised expression from taking over her face. *It's her! The woman in my dream! And it's not a pepperoni!*

The woman caught the look and asked, "Do I know you?"

"Oh, I'm sorry. You look so much like someone I know. I'm Sheridan, and you are?" Ever since she was a child, Sheila had wanted to be called Sheridan. For the life of her, her mother couldn't figure out why. A feeling of excitement stirred inside her using the fictitious name now.

"Ms. Bunson," she answered with a queenly air, as if announcing it to a room full of students, expecting them to all rise and repeat it in unison.

Sheila thought she was as frigid as a snooty character out of a Jane Austen book. "What are you drinking, Ms. Bunson?" she asked.

"A dirty martini. Certainly not the *best* I've ever had," she said with a scowl directed toward Vince.

"Oh, well then, guess I won't have *that*." Sheila stifled a laugh when catching Vince stick his tongue out at the woman. "Just give me a beer, please. That one on tap with the goat's head will do."

Beer was not her usual choice, but Sheila knew that if she drank anything else her tongue would loosen, and tonight, she needed to be sharp. She was determined to find out what this mysterious Ms. Bunson, who had appeared in her dreams and made Mildred want to quit, was up to, and now was her chance.

"I will have another," Ms. Bunson demanded, "except this time don't use so much Vermouth. Honestly," she said gruffly under her breath but loud enough for anyone eavesdropping to hear, "I can't get used to the incompetent bartenders, the hicks, and mostly the weirdos in Austin. This would never happen in Houston."

"Grrr," Vince growled with his back turned.

Sheila leaned in to try and read what was on the paper now sitting on top of her brief case.

"Business at the bar?" she asked, sipping on her beer nonchalantly.

Ms. Bunson groaned, "Yes, this company is so behind the times. But things will change when I'm in the driver's seat. That's for certain."

Sheila bit her lip. She wasn't sure what to say next, as she watched Ms. Bunson put the stapled papers back in the briefcase and closed it shut. "WHERE are the restrooms?" she bellowed.

Vince pointed the way, and when she was out of sight, he hurried back over to Sheila. "What a creepy woman…uh, right Sheridan?"

"Yeah, well, I like that name. Just go with it," she said with a smile of satisfaction. "But Vince, I fear she's worse than creepy. I'll explain later, but I've got to know what she's up to." Sheila opened the woman's briefcase and snatched the papers from it. "Quick, watch the door, and let me know when she's coming back."

Vince's eyes darted every way but upward, hoping no one else was watching the thief stealing right in front of him. He was so excited he didn't realize he was twisting a knot in the towel he held. He accidentally dropped it in the sudsy sink when he saw Ms. Bunson heading their way.

Before she even reached the bar, Ms. Bunson began complaining, "And another thing," she held her finger high in the air, "your restrooms are in a *horrible* state. I could barely get the toilet paper off the roll, and it took *forever* for the hot water to warm up."

Both hands now squeezing the water out of the drenched towel, Vince was determined to act cool. He was wrapped up in a web of espionage and clearly being tested. He nearly swooned with excitement.

"Hmm, that's too bad, I'm next." Sheila gave the disgruntled woman a sour face on her way to the restroom, the purse carrying the papers held tightly under her armpit. Behind Ms. Bunson's back, she mouthed to Vince, "Keep her busy."

Sitting on the toilet lid, she scanned the papers titled, "New Management," and the start date was tomorrow. A numerical list of steps to be taken flowed over to three full pages. Number one was in all caps: AXE THE ENTIRE FICTION DEPT.

Sheila gasped, astounded by the news and the similarities from her dreams: axe, the mole, Bunson and Bunyan. *But what about the pizza?* No time to figure that out now. Her blood was boiling, and she had to call Bernice, as this would affect her the most, being less than six months away from retiring.

A quick phone call made safely within the walls of the stall, and Sheila was back at the bar sitting next to the executioner, waiting for Bernice to arrive. Meanwhile, she would work to get the woman drunk and take it from there. "She's right, the restrooms suck!" she reported to the bartender.

"Well, Ms. Bunson," Sheila went in for the kill with a saccharine sweetness, "I can't let a savvy businesswoman like you go back to Houston thinking everything's bad about our town. Can I buy you the next martini?"

Ms. Bunson shot daggers at the bartender and smiled at Sheila; her eyes wickedly pleased to be proven right. "That should make things better."

Vince grudgingly slid a bowl of peanuts in front of her as a peace offering. He visualized her choking on one.

The third martini began to numb Ms. Bunson's tongue, and although her words were beginning to slur, it was quite clear that her intentions were bad. When Bernice arrived, Sheila nearly burst out laughing watching her waltz into the room in a gaudy yellow polka dotted dress and a fire-red Annie wig, lips and purse to match. She flopped down next to Ms. Bunson, her top-heavy breasts jiggling when she spoke, sounding like a woman right off the farm.

"Howdy, Vince!" she bellowed with such gusto, Ms. Bunson jerked.

"Hi, uh, ma'am," he managed to say, not sure what he should call Bernice. "What's your pleasure?"

"Oh, pleasure, huh? Serving up *pleasure*, are we?" she elbowed Ms. Bunson and gave her an exaggerated wink. "Just kidding, just kidding." She leaned in and studied Ms. Bunson's face. "Hmm, you're that woman on that movie.

What's it called? What's it called?" she asked with squinting eyes, expecting poor Vince to have an answer.

"I'm not sure what you're talking about." Ms. Bunson sat up straighter, her eyes lighting up waiting to hear what movie star she favored.

Sheila sat rigid and wide eyed wondering what Bernice was scheming and trying desperately not to laugh.

"The actress with the mole, that's it!" Bernice pounded the bar with her fist. "You know who I'm talkin' about."

"The wicked witch of the west?" Vince whispered to Sheila under his cupped hand just as she took a gulp of beer. Stifling the laugh, her mouth full, Sheila nearly spewed.

"Well, I've been told I look like that woman on *The Notebook*. She has a beauty mark just like mine," Ms. Bunson cooed, pursing her lips and brushing her hair back from her face, making sure that everyone saw the likeness on her chin. "My face is just a little fuller. More mature."

"Ahhh," Bernice looked closer. "That's a *beauty*. But I don't think it's supposed to have a hair sticking out of it. Otherwise, it's just a plain ole mole. Want me to pluck it?"

"Oh, good heavens, NO!"

"Well, if you change your mind, I have a pair of tweezers right here in my purse. Vince, I'll have what she's havin', and put her next one on me. I'm sittin' next to a movie star, by golly!"

Somehow whatever Bernice was doing seemed to work, because Ms. Bunson not only accepted her fourth martini, she also drank whatever Vince slipped in front of her. On Ms Bunson's second visit to the ladies' room, Sheila showed the papers to Bernice and then sneakily slipped them back inside the briefcase. Cool headed Bernice was on the case! Vince proudly announced he was all in, too.

When coaxed, Ms. Bunson revealed her plans to take

over the magazine and cockily waved around the flash drive she would be presenting to the staff the next morning. She said that Edward, the owner of the magazine had approved everything, and she had it all in writing. The very intoxicated Ms. Bunson not only spilled her guts, she spilled her last drink, and when she nearly fell off the barstool, Vince let someone else close the bar and carried the loose-lipped patron out the door. Bernice and Sheila hailed down a taxi and they all piled in with Ms. Bunson out cold in Vince's lap.

"What do we do now?" Sheila whispered. "This woman is about to ruin our lives and fire the entire fiction department. All nine of us!"

Vince covered Ms. Bunson's ear with his hand. "Well, you can't kill her, so let's take her to my friend's apartment. Ricardo's a former Chippendale dancer with a great mind for complicated situations. He'll know what to do."

Bernice grinned with excitement and elbowed Sheila, who was visibly dumbfounded and had no idea what a Chippendale was. Bernice gladly offered to explain. This whole thing was getting crazier by the minute, but there was no turning back. Their futures were at stake.

Ricardo opened the apartment door dressed in only a pair of boxers and a black bowtie around his neck. His entire body was a solid rock of masculinity, and his face looked like a young Arnold Schwarzenegger; he even had the gap between his front teeth. In his early sixties, the former stripper didn't have a wrinkle anywhere on his buffed and polished body. Bernice couldn't take her eyes off him. He carried Ms. Bunson to his bed, left her there and offered everyone milk and sponge cake. Gathered around the kitchen table, they told Ricardo the whole story and within minutes he had a plan.

"OK, so the word we're looking for here is sabotage. We

need to set this horrible woman up with something so damaging, she'll run back to Houston with her tail between her legs. I have the perfect plan." Ricardo picked up the phone and called his buddies.

A mere twenty minutes later, a knock was heard at the apartment door and when Ricardo opened it, five men, four with perfectly gorgeous physiques filed in. The last one wore a plaid shirt and was carrying a large professional camera with gear.

Bernice grabbed Sheila's arm and pulled her closer. "Well, there's your lumberjack, in flesh and blood."

Sheila looked at the man and smiled. He returned it. He didn't fit the description of a male dancer; the love handles were a dead giveaway. But he was nice looking, even in his thick beard, both ladies agreed.

Introductions were skipped, except for introducing the cameraman to the ladies. Cam, short for Campbell, worked for Ricardo's brother, a prominent film maker in town, and he was cool with offering his film expertise for the cause. He sat up a tripod to shoot the scene; another camera ready to aim dangled around his neck.

Ricardo sent Vince and the ladies to the hallway and ordered them to remain quiet. He asked Bernice if he could borrow her wig. He slapped it right over his balding head on his way to the bedroom where he picked up Ms. Bunson and brought her to the living room sofa. She mumbled something, opened her eyes, and smiled up at him. "Just a dream honey, a juicy one, too," he said, changing the inflection of his voice, pulling a mask over his eyes, and nodding at the cameraman to start rolling.

"Oh, goodie!" the words slipped from her sagging lips, as her head dropped forward onto his bare chest.

"Now!" Ricardo ordered, and when the music started,

the men, wearing black Zorro masks, began slowly grinding their hips, all in a semi-circle around Ms. Bunson.

Ms. Bunson opened her eyes and squealed again, "Oh, goodie!"

Cam stood stone-faced behind the camera, as hairless chests were exposed first, shirts seductively unbuttoned and thrown at Mrs. Bunson's feet. One by one they took turns slipping out of their pants down to only a thin strapped G-String, each one a different vibrant color. All together they wiggled their bottoms in her face, as they strutted their wares.

Bernice and Sheila were at first horrified, until one of the men grabbed Ms. Bunson's hand and pretended to slap his bottom with it. The scene was so comical, they had to move further back to keep their laughter from being heard.

"In all my wildest dreams, this is the wildest," Sheila whispered to a doubled-over Bernice. Vince was nearly crying he was laughing so hard. No one noticed the strange, almost painful, look on Cam's face.

"But look at Ms. Bunson, she's actually enjoying it," Bernice gasped. And at that moment, Ms. Bunson stood up and began chasing the men around the room, slapping every naked bottom she could see in her blinded drunkenness. Cam continued to shoot from the corner of the room and zoomed in closer when finally, the exhausted Ms. Bunson stumbled on top of one of the men, face first landing on his groin, her skirt lifted over her back with the help of Ricardo. A long run in her panty hose traveled slowly up her leg. Cam moved the camera closer in and filmed it. It was an especially arty final touch, everyone agreed with smiles and nods.

"She's out cold again," Ricardo concluded.

With that, Cam said in a stern low voice, "I think we have enough." He gathered up his equipment and sat down in front of his laptop. He removed the flash drive from the camera. His job was to replace it with the one in Ms. Bunson's briefcase, while Sheila located the hotel fob with the room number in her purse. Ms. Bunson was carried back outside to the taxi and taken to her hotel.

When they got inside the elevator, she woke up to Ricardo holding her in his arms.

"What the hell!" Ms. Bunson screamed. "Put me down!"

"Sure thing, lady," he quickly obeyed.

"Who *are* you, and *what* am I doing in this elevator with you?" She shoved Ricardo into the moving wall and braced herself up in the opposite corner – her shoe in her hand held up high as a weapon.

"Lady, you were so drunk, I was asked to take you to your hotel room. I think rather than beat me with a shoe, you owe me a thank you." He stepped forward and put out his hand.

"Back off buster, or I'll make a bigger gap between those teeth when I whack you with these steel supported heels!"

"No problem." Ricardo's hands flew up in surrender until the elevator stopped on the next floor. He handed over the key to Ms. Bunson, and before the doors closed shut, he stuck his head back inside and said in a sexy tone, "Oh, goodie!"

The confused and wretched look on Ms. Bunson's face was priceless, and Ricardo enjoyed describing it to Sheila who was waiting in the hotel lobby chatting away with Cam. The final step to the plan was in place, and Ricardo bid them goodnight. The four dancers were on their way to "Le Bare la Boom" with Bernice driving them all in her minivan. She promised she'd attend the company meeting but would definitely be late for work. Vince and Ricardo both went home, pleased with themselves. Sheila and Cam shared a taxi back to their cars. Cam rushed off to handle some other business after asking for her phone number, his excuse being, he had to know how it ended. Sheila hoped there was more to it than just that.

Sleep was the last thing on Sheila's mind when she arrived at her place long after her usual bedtime. The bulk of the evening was spent searching online for anything relating to a certain cameraman that worked for a certain movie maker in a certain city in Texas. By the time she dozed off, she was certain she was barking up the right tree when she learned he was single with no ex-wives in his past and nearly the same age. But what did make her uncertain was who that certain someone was related to. Things might be getting a little more complicated than she thought. She certainly hoped not.

The company meeting was to be held at noon the following day, and the flash drive Ms. Bunson carried was to be viewed by everyone in attendance on the overhead projector screen. A major take-over was in order, and besides wiping out the fiction department, there were other changes that were quite disturbing; changes that would destroy the integrity of the magazine and its original intent. Little did Ms. Bunson know that the flash drive contained something entirely different.

The first to arrive at work, Sheila went straight to Mildred's office. When she entered, Mildred was in her chair asleep, face down on the desk, her arms limp by her side. She had stayed there all night long. "Mildred, Mildred, wake up."

Mildred raised her weary head. A sticky note stuck to her chin. The heavy mascara and eyeliner she wore daily had dripped down her face, and she looked like a member of a Kiss cover band with a hangover. Sheila handed her a box of tissue and wasted no time getting to the point.

"I know what's going on, and I know we're all being fired, and it's happening today," she said emphatically.

"You do? Oh, Sheila, I am so upset. This company is my life. How could Edward let this happen to his own magazine?"

"Supposedly that evil woman, Ms. Bunson, is his sister-in-law, and my understanding is that he has been severely depressed since his wife died, and he has these lapses where he goes back into time and is reliving his youth. He probably has no idea what's going on. That horrible woman has him on some very strong anti-depressants and sleep medication."

"And you learned all this, *how?*" Mildred gave Sheila the look she usually gave Bernice.

"Never mind that…for now."

"Well, that explains why I can't seem to reach him on the phone. But these changes will ruin us. I'm beside myself."

"Don't be, we have a plan in the making. Today at the meeting, she'll reveal her true self. Hopefully the Vice President will step in and at least postpone this until we can get to the bottom of it."

"Sheila, the VP knows about it. He quit yesterday."

"Well, then we'll just have to fight her ourselves! By the way, what are they serving for lunch at this meeting?"

"Pizza," Mildred said. "Why?"

"Just curious…I haven't had breakfast." Sheila held her hand to her forehead and smiled for a reason Mildred would never know.

Only Sheila and Bernice knew what was about to happen in the meeting room. But where was Bernice? The entire staff of forty-two employees had arrived, happy as clams anticipating pizza delivery, but Bernice was not among them. Ms. Bunson took the stage without delay and began explaining that necessary changes would be made to the company and the magazine's mission would no longer be about women, health tips, and how to feel younger at any age, knitting, education, etcetera. And the fiction department would be the biggest change of all. The primary focus would be on movie stars, glamour, risqué stories, hot topics, and Ms. Bunson would become the new Editor-in-Chief. "In other words," she stressed, "no more average woman nonsense!"

The employees began a chorus of murmurs, shaking their heads, looking at each other in confusion. Ms. Bunson had not yet dropped the bomb about firing the entire fiction department. She glowered at Sheila who sat nervously waiting for the axe to fall.

"Oh my gosh, she recognizes me," Sheila gasped. *Where the heck are you, Bernice? I can't do this alone.*

Pizza came in twenty boxes, carried in the arms of two teens who stacked them on the table. A third teen rolled in a cooler full of canned soda pop and juices. Innocently, they were eager to fill their plates full, as Ms. Bunson ordered the lights dimmed for the presentation to begin. Bernice crept up behind Sheila and gave her a fright. At the same time, in the darkened room, two figures slipped in unnoticed from behind the crowd.

The presentation was not the scene in Ricardo's living room, as Sheila expected. Muted, the numbered changes were presented one by one in huge letters across the screen while Ms. Bunson stood to the right waving a pointer stick, reading aloud. She and Bernice were aghast that their plan had not worked.

"Something's wrong, Bernice," Sheila whispered. "I learned something last night that has me confused. Maybe the reason why the thumb drive isn't the one Cam filmed is because, well, because he didn't exchange it with the original as we planned. He and Ms. Bunson may be in cahoots together. They're related!"

"What? Say that again," Bernice bent over and whispered hoarsely in her ear. But when the part about firing her entire department came across the screen, Bernice ignored Sheila, bucked up, and began chanting, "Not NO, but hell NO!"

Sheila bowed her head and mumbled, "We're doomed."

Within seconds, the entire room joined her. "Not NO, but hell NO!" Ms. Bunson stood self-righteously annoyed and rolled her eyes. Then, out of the dim light two men walked up in front of the screen. To their surprise, Edward, the gentle and distinguished elderly owner of the magazine raised his hand to quiet the crowd. Cam, the cameraman in blue plaid stood next to him without his camera, his hand on the old man's shoulder. The employees came to a hush when they recognized their leader. Sheila and Bernice were simply gobsmacked. "That's what I was trying to tell you, Bernice. I think we've been sabotaged by a man in plaid."

"Everyone, everyone," Edward shouted in a weak voice and then paused as if he had forgotten what to say. Cam whispered something in his ear. "Oh yes, oh yes," he continued with much stronger vocal cords, "there will not be any changes! None whatsoever!" He turned to Ms. Bunson and wagged his finger. "Brenda, shame on you!"

Relieved that Cam was one for the team, Sheila smiled

and waved wildly across the room to get his attention. His grin at seeing her said it all.

Ms. Bunson puffed out her chest. "We shall see, Edward," she countered and stuck her tongue out at him. "You are unfit to run this company!"

Edward laughed, "Oh yeah?" He walked over to the table, grabbed a slice of pizza off someone's plate and threw it at her, hitting his pompous sister-in-law smack dab on the forehead.

A bleating, "Ohh!" was heard from the onlookers as they gazed upon the horrified Ms. Bunson and Ed standing there defying her as if they were kids throwing snowballs. He had no doubt slipped back in time, again.

"You're all fired! Including you, Ed!" Ms. Bunson announced on the microphone.

Bernice stood on her toes and yelled, "Food fight!" and flung a whole pizza at Ms. Bunson that wobbled right past her mole. The next one she threw didn't miss. The room went wild, and everyone began hurling pizza slices all around. Raucous laughter was heard above Ms. Bunson's screams. Someone shook up a can of soda and began spraying the others. Within seconds pop tops were flicked open and the room began to shower sticky liquid everywhere.

Cam slipped away, dodging pizza on his way toward the computer still playing the presentation. Sheila followed him. He pulled out the flash drive and inserted his own. With the volume on high, "Oh, goodie!" resonated throughout the room. The staff stopped the food fight and with pepperoni, olives, and carbonated fluids dripping from their clothing and their astounded faces, all their attention was directed toward Ms. Bunson in action on the giant screen. In the sudden stillness, Edward started laughing. He sounded like a donkey, slapping his thighs, and snorting through his nose. The entire group joined in as Ms. Bunson stood paralyzed, staring at herself spanking the shiny naked bottoms of a room full of men in leather and satin G-Strings.

Bernice grabbed Edward's hand, pulled him over to Sheila and Cam and said, "I'm taking Ed out for a drink. Join me at Lucy's?"

They both looked over at Edward who was smiling goofily at Bernice as if he had been shot with Cupid's arrow, gazing admiringly at the chunk of pizza stuck to her chest. Cam grabbed Sheila's hand, and the four of them scurried out the door. In seconds they were skipping down the sidewalk, pulling the laughing Edward all the way.

At the bar, Vince served drinks while listening attentively to their story and basking in their thanks. Edward was given a Shirley Temple disguised as a mixed drink.

"Are you OK, uncle?" Cam asked, patting Edward on the back.

"I haven't felt this good in a long time." Edward's eyes teared up. "It's good to see you Cam…and your friends. I've been a lonely man without my Gilda."

"Oh, so that's it. You're Edward's nephew," Bernice exclaimed, "which makes you…oh no, please don't tell me that Ms. Bunson is your mother!" The possible connection made her look and feel extremely uncomfortable.

Sheila suddenly felt ashamed that she had entertained the idea that Cam was teaming up with Ms. Bunson. But she was relieved that Bernice didn't hear her try to tell her that earlier in the meeting room.

"No, she's not my mother. Ms. Bunson, or Aunt Brenda, is Gilda's, Edward's late wife's, stepsister. As you know, Gilda was the originator of the magazine. My father is Gilda's brother."

"A bit confusing, but I get it. You are family. But how could you be so bold to film your own aunt like that?" Bernice asked.

"My step aunt," he emphasized, "is and has been, let's say, a thorn in our side for many years."

"A pain in the ass!" Edward roared.

Cam continued, "I don't think I would have had the courage if you hadn't told me what she was up to. My Aunt Gilda loved her magazine, and this takeover would have devastated her." Cam reached over and patted Edward's back. "I'm sorry I had to get you involved, Uncle Ed, but I had no choice. And I'm sorry I had to resort to using the movie we made. Aunt Brenda is incorrigible."

"You did the right thing. The magazine was my Gilda's pride and joy," Edward mumbled, bowing his head, a tear dropping into his glass. "I think this drink is making me a little silly."

Everyone smiled at each other and gathered around the old man with hugs and kisses. Vince lovingly plopped a fresh cherry in his drink. Edward opportunely rested his head on Bernice's pepperoni scented bosom.

⁌⁊

The magazine continued as it had for forty years. Edward turned the publishing company over to Bernice, but she would not under any circumstances sleep with him, even though she moved into his mansion.

Vince landed a job managing the swankiest nightclub in town where the elite hang out. He puts the material he gathers from the wealthy busybodies into stories and sells them to gossip magazines as a freelance writer under the pen name, *Invincible.* On the side, he dabbles in blackmail.

As for Ms. Bunson, well, the home movie Ricardo created with Ms. Bunson as the star, went viral and now together, they all perform the same routine in male strip shows across the nation. The dancers call themselves *Bunson's Buns* and believe it or not, they named the show, "Oh, Goodie!"

Cam and Sheila married after several months of heavy dating. Cam confessed that he had always wanted to be a lumberjack, when in fact, he really just loved the smell of freshly cut wood. Sheila admitted that she had always hated plaid and had secretly desired to edit stories about men, for a change. Edward's wedding gift to the couple provided enough funds to help Cam buy a lumberyard in Oregon, where Sheila created and published a new magazine called *Men in Paisley*. In their home built entirely with logs, she lovingly filled her new husband's closet with dozens of colorful paisley shirts. Not completely insensitive to his love for the checkered pattern, she had all his plaid flannel shirts made into baby blankets for their upcoming baby boy, Paul, named after, you guessed it, that big burly guy with the axe that innocently started this whole darn thing.

A DIFFERENT PATH

*I*nstead of taking the usual trail with the crunchy pebbles, Cara took a different path home: a less traveled one with clumps of unruly grass and rocks scattered sporadically under foot. As she moved along it, she heard creatures scurrying within the thick brush surrounding her. *Rattlesnakes?* A co-worker had recently found one leisurely lying on his window ledge, its evil eye transfixed on his spoiled, fat cat. She fought off the urge to run because today she would not allow anything, not even an ugly flat-faced reptile toting a silly baby rattle, ruin the euphoria that had led her to a relaxing walk in the woods.

Cara was experiencing a rare sense of adventure brought on by two amazing events, all happening within a week. It started with a job opportunity, a chance to work alongside a pastry chef in the beautiful Fairlie-Poplar historic district of Atlanta. A dream come true, but seven-hundred miles away meant the end of her relationship with her boyfriend, Rusty.

A decision this major required guidance, and she knew that the best person to talk to would be her older, sensible sister, Brynn. In preparation for their talk, Brynn knew that baking brought out the best in Cara, and the smell and taste of freshly baked cookies did wonders for stress relief. So, upon Cara's arrival, Brynn had her trapped in the kitchen stirring dough and spilling her guts.

Brynn's questions always made sense, and Cara's answers came honestly, in between licks of the spoon.

"Trips?"

"No, we've never traveled together…anywhere."

"Deep talks?"

"No, not really. We've never talked in depth about our families, much less about children. I get the impression Rusty doesn't like children, though."

"Do you argue?"

"Rarely, because there's nothing really to argue about." Cara went on to say that they read different books, listened to different music, and after watching a movie they would only discuss the acting and nothing about the plot. Four months of dating ran something like a bus schedule: Friday night dinner and a movie, Sunday church followed by brunch, and forget weekdays when Rusty spent most of his free time with a sixteen-piece army on a black and white checkered board while Cara stayed home and caught up on her favorite romance novels.

"How about intimacy, you know…sex?"

With that topic, the laughter poured out of Cara when she told Brynn that the closest they ever came to intimacy was when Rusty drank too many martinis and fell asleep naked on her chest. She had stayed awake, fully clothed, rigid beneath him until he finally awoke, groggy and disoriented. Embarrassed, she let him leave wondering if anything had happened between them.

The giggling came to a halt when Cara begrudgingly

divulged, "I'm the only twenty-nine-year-old virgin left on the planet."

Older sisters take counseling their siblings seriously, and Brynn did not miss a beat. Over "fresh from the oven" chocolate chip cookies and an ice-cold glass of milk, she managed to get Cara to admit that the real reason she carried on with Rusty was because he was the only boyfriend she'd ever had, and with no other prospects, her crazy biological clock was spinning wildly out of control. In a final breakthrough, Cara agreed that it all boiled down to one thing – she was afraid of ending up alone.

Bolstered by Brynn's cheers, Cara made the decision to take the job. When she told Rusty, he seemed to have no opinion whatsoever and offered her a simple congratulatory hug. Sure, it bruised her ego, but it also made it easier to accept that their relationship had run its course, probably grown stale from the routine dating. They would continue seeing each other for the next three weeks, at which time they would part forever. With no more excuses, Cara promised herself she would not let fear get in the way of a potentially fabulous future.

As easy as pie, everything was running like clockwork until unexpectedly, without provocation, Rusty asked her to marry him. Never in a billion years could Cara have predicted anything so monumental, and she was quite surprised how quickly and without any further thought she rejected Atlanta and said yes to his sudden proposal. All of Brynn's inspiring words of wisdom flew right out the window.

But now, here in the woods surrounded by nature and all alone with her own private thoughts, unwanted questions rose to the surface. Naturally suspicious, Cara wondered if Rusty had proposed because of the large inheritance money she would receive when her grandmother, inching toward a hundred, finally surrendered to the light.

"And wait a minute, how did he guess my ring size?" she questioned aloud. She owned only one ring, a special fourteen-caret gold Irish Claddagh that she wore traditionally on the right hand with the heart facing outward to show that she was open to love. But he couldn't have determined her size from that. She had lost that ring three months ago.

"And hold your horses...has he ever said, I love you?" she blurted, startling a plump dove on a low-lying branch overhead. Grateful for the disruption, she stopped in her tracks and watched the frightened, heavy-breasted bird flutter clumsily toward the sky. "Sometimes I wish I could fly away, too." The poor bird crashed into a clump of leaves but tumbled safely onto a limb. "Yeah, that would be me alright," she grumbled.

Cara shook her fists in the air and scolded herself for letting rambling annoyances ruin her happy mood. "Who cares! Love, love, love, blah, blah, blah! I will not die an old maid!" Holding the ring up to the sunlight again, she announced loudly, "Mrs. Cara Gifford." Before any more doubt could fill her head, she took off in a hurry and sprinted the rest of the way home.

✂

She was humming, "Sadie, Sadie, married lady," when she approached her apartment and spotted her sister sitting by the pool playing with her cell phone. As usual, Brynn glowed in her mother's beauty and smooth olive skin. Cara took after her father with his double chin and eyes so close together, she was grateful to hide them behind dark rimmed glasses. She felt lucky to have her mother's full lips and straight, white teeth, which she earned after six grueling years with braces.

"Hey, Brynn. Come on up," she yelled from the balcony above.

Brynn had always been a good sister, but there was a life-long history of jealousy that Cara just could not seem to shake. It grew worse over the years watching Brynn emerge as an artist with her own studio, and shortly after, marry her gynecologist. She lived in a beautiful mini mansion that her husband, George, could easily afford. Unlike Rusty, who was an accountant with a small nonprofit organization. Along with her job as a cake baker and decorator, they would struggle financially in her tiny apartment until the inheritance money was disbursed. Whenever that would be.

As she stood there gazing down at Brynn, she panicked. How in the world could she explain her sudden decision to marry Rusty? All sensibility was lost the moment he popped the question. Frantically pulling the engagement ring from her finger, she hid it deep in the back of her panty drawer.

Brynn entered the apartment talking to her husband on the cell phone and hugged Cara with one arm. "Give me a second," she whispered. "George is telling me an interesting story."

"Sure," Cara whispered back and went to put on a pot of tea. From her kitchen in the small apartment, she could hear her sister say, "You're kidding. Are you sure?" And then she said under her breath, "Oh my, God! Dad was right all along."

Cara tiptoed to the doorway and stood watching Brynn facing the wall, whispering into the phone. When she hung up, Brynn turned around and was startled at seeing her sister standing there staring at her expressionless. Throughout their childhood, Cara often appeared creepily out of nowhere, and Brynn had still not gotten used to it. The whistle from the tea kettle interrupted the awkward moment.

"Oh great, you're making tea. Hope you have some of those yummy cupcakes left to go with it." Brynn dropped her phone back into the big pocket of her art smock, brushed past her sister, and patted her on the behind. "How are you doing, sis?"

"I'm fine. Did you just come from your studio?"

She looked down at the paint-blotched smock. "Yes, I guess I did. These things are so comfortable I forget to take them off. Love these giant pockets. I could fit a chimpanzee in this one," she laughed. Brynn loved to laugh at her own corny remarks and along with the goofy faces she made, Cara couldn't help but chuckle.

Cara turned to pour the tea. "Sounded like a serious phone call. Care to share?"

"Spare a square? Ha, ha! I love that scene in Seinfeld. Remember when…"

"I hope nothing is wrong. You sounded pretty serious."

"Yes, well, I was just told something…something disturbing."

"Really? What might that be?" Cara cringed, wondering if somehow she knew about the engagement.

Brynn sat down and propped her feet up on a chair. "Well, I'm not sure where to start, but it's about your boyfriend," she said, raising her eyebrows over the top of the steaming cup.

Oh dear, she knows, Cara thought, trying not to show her surprise. Here comes the thrashing! "OK, what about him?"

"George said that he saw him with a guy at Grover Park. A very thin guy with an impressively large nose. George said he looked a little like Keith Richards. Do you know who he is?"

"Of course, that's Carl. He's Rusty's best friend. They play chess there all the time. Gosh, I think about two or three times a week."

"Hmmm," Brynn hummed, sliding her finger around the rim of the ceramic cup. "George just recently started running in that park. He happened to be running there this morning when he saw them. They were not in the area where all the chess folks meet up." She stalled to take a sip. "They were in the middle of the park, in a secluded area."

"And?"

"How long have you known Carl?"

"Oh, I don't know. I guess since I met Rusty, but I've only seen him a few times. They also work in the same building." Cara, easily irritated and feeling the last of the earlier bliss evaporate, cut to the chase. "What exactly is your point?"

Brynn, looking profoundly serious, put the cup down and clasped her hands together. "This is not easy to say, and if it came from another source other than my husband, I prob-ably would be laughing by now. But, since it was George, well, I have to believe him. He said that he saw Rusty's arm around Carl."

"So?" Cara sat back in the chair, frowning.

"Then...he saw him kiss him." Brynn's nose wrinkled up as if she had smelled sour milk.

"WHAT?" Cara shrilled, wrinkling her nose as if she had been tricked into smelling the sour milk, too.

"Yeah, he kissed Carl. Not a peck on the cheek, or on the head, but a kiss...you know, a real smooch." Brynn puckered her lips and made a loud smacking sound.

"You've got to be kidding!" Cara stood up and went to the sink where she unconsciously poured out her tea.

Keeping her back to her sister, she said, "You know George could have been mistaken. I mean, runner's high and all, maybe he thought he saw them kissing, or maybe he thought he saw Rusty, when in fact it wasn't him at all."

"Honey, George knows what he saw. He was very clear about it, and he *did* second guess himself. That's why he stood behind a tree and watched a little while longer. I know he must have felt weird spying like that, but he said that he had to make sure because of you. You know George, he doesn't joke around. Why, he doesn't even talk about the women patients that he sees naked every day, and I bet there are some funny stories behind that. Your brother-in-law is a pretty serious dude and besides, who could miss Rusty's red hair?"

"I just don't believe it," Cara bemoaned, catching her warped frown in the reflection of the spoon. "Especially, after last night."

"What happened last night?" Brynn eased up from behind and placed her arm around Cara to console her from the blow she had just delivered.

"He asked me to marry him."

"What?" Brynn quickly looked down at Cara's hand, relieved to not find a ring. "Phew, for a second there I thought you told him yes. That's a relief! We're all so excited about your new job in Atlanta. Really a great break, honey."

Cara started to tell her sister the truth, but she couldn't. It was all so icky now. Tainted. She refused to believe that George knew what he saw. This must be a mistake. It has to be! She slipped out of Brynn's embrace. "I really find this hard to believe." The old familiar jealousy came from out of nowhere, and in a sudden rage, she threw the cup into the sink, shattering it into pieces. A sizable chunk flew up and hit her in the arm. "Ouch!" she yelled, cupping her hand over the cut.

"Oh, Cara! Let me see, let me see!" Brynn pulled her sister's hand away from the wound.

Cara drew back from her and cried out, "Haven't you done enough? Just because you have the perfect life, the perfect husband, the perfect house, do you have to ruin my perfect day? You're so goddamn pretty with perfect hair, a perfect career, and I'm the ugly duckling making just enough to get by, and now I finally have a man that wants to marry me. Sure, he's boring and barely makes a living. And he's a Republican! I wouldn't put it past you to sabotage my future just for that reason alone!" Cara stopped just long enough to catch the tears forming in Brynn's eyes before she turned away and hurried to the living room.

Brynn followed her. "There is no truth to anything you just said, Cara. I told you this because I don't want you to get hurt, and you know I love you. And there's another thing. Dad has always thought that Rusty was leaning toward the other side. Your own father! I can't help but agree. Especially now!"

"Go home, Brynn. Go home to your castle and tell King George he needs to see an eye doctor!" Cara ran to her bedroom and locked the door behind her.

"I'm sorry, sis," Brynn spoke to the closed door. "I'm really sorry. I know it hurts, but just think, you have a whole life ahead of you, your new job, your..."

"Shut up!" Cara screamed into the pillow.

"I'll be at my studio if you need me." Brynn said glumly. Knowing her sister would pout for some time, she snatched up a cupcake and left the apartment.

Cara rolled from side to side in the bed squeezing a pillow between her thighs and another she clutched like a child who was holding onto her dad's neck for dear life, knowing he was about to throw her in the pool for the first time. She waited until she calmed down to call Rusty.

Rusty picked up on the fifth ring, just before Cara almost gave up. "Hello, Rusty Gifford here," he said cheerfully. Cara generally tolerated his voice filled with cracks and squeaks, like a boy in puberty, but now she heard it as bicycle brakes squealing, and it made that incessant ringing in her ears louder.

"Hi, it's me."

"Yeah, I was just talking about you."

"Oh, really?" Cara sat up taller.

"Yeah, I'm here with Carl. I told him the good news."

Cara slumped. "Have you told anyone else?"

"Not yet, but I will," he teased.

"Well, I'd rather you didn't tell anyone else. I'd like to have a formal dinner party and announce it that way. OK with you?"

"Well sure, that sounds nice." Rusty muffled the phone and said something to Carl.

"By the way, did you guys play chess today?" Cara asked, using a candy-coated voice that did not sound like her own.

"We did. And he beat the heck out of me. He's getting better and better," Rusty boasted. "Of course, he has been taught by the best."

"I know, I've heard that about you. Someday I'll have to learn the game. You two seem to enjoy it so much." And then Cara went in for the kill. "Where'd you play this time?"

"At Grover Park, our favorite place. You know, in that crazy chess area where all the weirdos hang out."

"Yeah, I heard about that," she said slowly, not sure what to say next. "I should probably come and watch you play sometime."

"Nah. You'd hate it. We're slow and sometimes it takes twenty minutes to make one move. Besides that, I'd get nervous if you were there and would probably make the wrong play. It gets pretty intense."

"I can only imagine. Hey, did you happen to run into George?"

"George, your brother-in-law?"

"Only George I know."

"Why would I run into him?"

"Oh, just curious. My sister told me that he runs that park a lot now because of its new trails. Matter of fact, she said he was there this morning. You must have just missed him."

"Maybe, uh, well, I need to get back to my office to look over some reports." Rusty's voice was rushed, eager to get off the phone. "By the way, I can't make it to church next Sunday. Explain later. Bye, bye."

"Uh, OK…but what about brunch?" her voice seeped into the silence of the dead phone.

Neither were good with salutations or closings, and perhaps it was her imagination, but he sure seemed hesitant to chat after she said George had been to the park. Still, this was not enough proof, and she resented Brynn for believing her husband without fully interrogating him. The anger she experienced earlier returned. She looked down at the gash in her arm and started licking the blood like a cat licking a dead bird. Her body trembled when a disturbing childhood memory came to mind.

At the time, Brynn was sixteen, and her very first date was standing at the front door. Cara watched them from the top of the stairs. The poor teen could barely talk he was so smitten by Brynn's cuteness. Brynn walked him into the living room to meet her parents. A wave of jealousy poured over Cara and before she knew it, she had slipped out the back door with a raw egg in her hand. Sneaking around the side of the house, she spotted a dead Cardinal on the ground beneath the kitchen window. The stupid bird had been crashing into his reflection in the glass every day that week. Just as her mother had feared, it finally banged its head one too many times and broke its neck. She picked it up by its beak and tossed it on the front passenger's seat of the boy's car. Smashing the egg on his windshield was no longer an exciting idea, so she put it in the mailbox. No one could have enjoyed more than her hearing Brynn scream when she sat on the decaying carcass.

The satisfaction from that prank and many before it, wore off quickly until the next time, and the next time, and over the years, Cara had a long list of tricks she had pulled on her sister. It wasn't until lately, remembering them began to disturb her conscience.

After applying Peroxide to the wound, she grabbed her car keys and decided to take a drive.

⚎

Rusty's office was in a small, two-story brick building not far from Grover's Park. She cruised around the parking lot until she spotted his car. But when she tried to enter the building, the door was locked. On a whim, she walked three blocks over to the park. It was nearly dusk, and folks were still lingering under the dim lights, some playing chess, others intently observing. She scanned the area with no sign of her fiancé or his big-nose buddy.

"Where is the trail to the center of the park?" she thought to ask a woman in the group busily stringing up her bootlaces.

"Just walk past that doggy poop bag holder and you'll see the sign. But, if I were you, I wouldn't walk too far. What happens after dark in there may not be something you want to witness."

The man next to her laughed and said, "She's right about that."

"Thanks, I won't be too long. I'm more concerned about rattlesnakes."

"Rattlesnakes?"

She wasn't sure what she was doing, but morbid curiosity was in the driver's seat. She walked slowly, stopping to listen about every ten steps. As she got deeper into the woods, she heard a groaning sound. A bear? She started to turn back, but the groaning got louder and more sporadic, definitely human. It came from beyond a clump of bushes to her left. She moved in closer, crouched down, and peered through the leafy stems. In the fading sun it was hard to make out the shapes, but it looked like two people dancing in each other's arms. With each erratic move came sharp, low sounding, grunts.

The dancing stopped and a voice whispered harshly in her direction. "Don't move!"

Cara froze. Suddenly, her phone buzzed in her pocket. Relieved it was on vibrate, she yanked it out of her fanny pack and saw that it had automatically called the last number she had dialed. She heard a ring come from beyond the shrubs. Her eyes widened. The second ring resonated against her ear, and a third rang from within the woods, followed by a voice, "Shit!" A short pause, and then, "It's Cara!"

"Don't answer it," a male's voice shrieked.

"Think I'm crazy?"

Trembling, Cara held her breath, ended the call and

walked quickly out of the woods just as dark fell. When she exited the park and hurried past the chess players, a woman called out glibly, "Did you find any rattlesnakes?"

"Matter of fact, I did, and I think it's mating season!"

From a block away, Cara could still hear laughter from the park. She was surprised by her witty comeback and wondered how she was able to say it with such ease. Brynn had always been the one with clever one-liners, not her. She caught herself gloating.

When she reached her car, she sat behind the steering wheel thinking about what to do next. Resigned to accepting the awful truth, it occurred to her that she should make things right with Brynn, but she was still too angry and now too appalled to do anything but go home and take a long hot shower. One thing she knew for sure, Rusty and Carl must be punished.

Feeling refreshed in a bathrobe, a thick towel wrapped around her wet head, a hot cup of tea at her lips, a plan began to formulate; one that would take a lot of courage. The kind of courage she never had but wanted more than anything in the world. She would talk it over with Brynn.

❖

Several days later Cara called Rusty. "I hate to tell you this, knowing it might hurt your feelings, but my dad doesn't care for you. I'm afraid if we announce the wedding, he won't pay for it. So, instead of ruffling his feathers, and since neither of us has the funds for a big ceremony, why don't we elope?"

Rusty cleared his throat, and Cara thought she could hear his teeth grinding. "I've only seen your dad maybe three times since we met. How could he draw that conclusion so easily?"

"I don't know, but he has, and when he gets an idea in his head, it sticks. I remember one time…"

"Uh, Cara, not that it matters. I mean, I don't care if you are rich or poor, but will this affect your inheritance? I sure don't want to mess things up for you. I mean, well, you know. It's an awful lot of money to pass up on account of me."

"Oh no. My grandmother doesn't feel the same way. It will be fine, but it will be easier on my family if we did it this way." Cara realized that she was in some twisted way, enjoying the ruse.

"Well then," Rusty sighed, "I'll do whatever you want. What's the plan?"

"I've got tickets to Las Vegas for next Saturday and we're scheduled to be married at four o'clock. And for your wedding gift, I also have a ticket for your best man, Carl."

"Oh, Cara. You are too good to me. What about you? Are you bringing your sister?"

"She's meeting us there. Matter of fact, she bought the tickets, the hotel rooms, and everything. We'll fly back Sunday in time for us to get back to work first thing Monday morning."

"It sounds crazy, but I like it!"

"Oh, and Rusty, here's the best part. My grandmother is going to give me my inheritance right after we get back. She says she doesn't want us living in this little, run-down apartment. She said that she'll handle my dad, and all will be just perfect."

"Wow, this is working out very nicely. I suppose I'll need to break the news to my mother. She'll hate living alone."

"Oh yes, I forgot you live with your mother." Add that to

the list, she thought. I've never even met his mother! She took a deep breath and proceeded to place the final nail in the coffin. "Listen, I think you should quit that lousy job and play with *me* for a while. We'll take one cruise after another, you and me and the love boat, baby!"

"I, I couldn't quit...right away. I mean...."

Cara shoved the phone under the sofa pillow just in case he could hear her sniveling. "Oh, suddenly you have some scruples, or maybe you just don't want to leave your little boyfriend?" She brought it back to her ear and demanded, "I insist!"

"Well, of course, if you insist. After all, you *are* the queen."

"No, dear, you *are*..., oops, well that's not right now, is it?" Cara was enjoying the new wit that she had recently acquired. She was also reveling in the power; the power of punishing the guilty, instead of the innocent. "Better let you go. We have a lot to do, and you have a boss to call. I'll see you at the airport Saturday morning at seven o'clock sharp. Bye, bye!"

Cara imagined Rusty standing there stunned in the wake of the exciting news and then rushing to Carl's office to tell him the latest plans. She had played her hand well, and everything was on target. Thanks to Brynn.

She put the phone down and turned to her sister. "I can't believe you are so eager to help me. You've never ever done anything hurtful in your entire life. You're not like me." Cara reached out for her hand. "I haven't been the best sister to you, Brynn. Are you sure about this?"

"Yes, I am, and you know, maybe it's time I help out my little sis. I've always wanted to be closer to you. This could be a start. Besides, I'm so glad you gave me back my charm bracelet after all these years. It meant a lot to me when we were kids. I thought it was gone forever. But you…you found it, and wow…"

"I didn't find it. I stole it from you. I was…I was awful. Jealous. Rotten." And with that confession out in the open, Cara poured her heart out with a string of guilty admissions.

The rest of the week crept by like the days before a root canal, and when Saturday morning finally arrived, Cara had almost lost her nerve until she saw Rusty and Carl standing close together in the ticketing area at the airport. They were so close, their Hawaiian shirts melded into one big garden of delight. Wedging her body in between them, in her bright pink dress, she took them by surprise.

"This is just too exciting," Carl yelped, and when he leaned over to hug her, the pendant at the end of his necklace slipped out of his low-buttoned shirt and hit Cara right in the eye.

"Ow," she flinched, looking up to see what hit her.

"Oh, oh, I'm sorry," Carl whined, grabbing the necklace, and quickly stuffing it back inside his shirt. His face reddened when he glanced over at Rusty who seemed to be trying his best not to scowl.

"I'm fine." Cara pulled on her eyelid. "That's a heck of a piece of jewelry you're wearing. College ring?" she asked, posing the question innocently, knowing quite well that what she just saw was her gold Irish ring.

"No, but it's *very* special. My girlfriend gave it to me," Carl said, his wide fake smile revealing his glistening gums.

"I didn't know you had a girlfriend. We could have

invited her, too. How sweet. What's her name?" Cara was now more than ever in the mood to complete the scheme.

"Uh," apparently searching all through his pea brain for a name, Carl blurted out, "Misty, Musty, I mean… Dusty! Yeah…Dusty."

"Dusty, oh that's cute, rhymes with Rusty. Does she also have red hair?"

"Cara," Rusty interrupted, having twitchily watched the exchange, "shouldn't we be checking in?"

"No, we have lots of time." Cara sneered, enjoying the fretful look on her future husband's face. But suddenly losing the will to interrogate poor terrified Carl any further, she agreed, "You're right, let's get in line."

It was hard sitting in the middle of the two connivers for the three-hour flight to Las Vegas. Cara could feel the tension between them and finally asked Rusty if he would move to an empty seat so that she could sprawl out. He suggested that they swap seats instead so that she could be near the aisle, and when she responded with an emphatic "NO!" accompanied by a low growl, he reluctantly moved to the back of the plane.

Carl pulled the airline magazine from the pocket in front of him and pretended to be interested in his read. Cara turned her head and pretended to sleep. When the flight attendant asked for drink orders, Cara ordered a double bourbon on the rocks for herself and offered to buy a drink for the best man. She figured that a criminal facing an execution was entitled to a final drink of his choice. When the drinks arrived, she toasted exuberantly to Rusty and Dusty.

By the time the plane landed, they each had three drinks under their belt, and Carl was a train wreck after Cara had spent most of the trip sharing intimate details of her alleged sex life with Rusty. It had been extremely helpful using naughty bits from "Fifty Shades of Grey." In fact, the woman sitting across the aisle, apparently eavesdropping, and enjoying every sordid detail, spurred Cara on with a nod of approval. When the flight attendant asked what she would like to drink, the woman answered, pointing directly to Cara, "I'll have what she's having."

In the taxi, Cara gave the driver directions to the chapel. He looked at her questionably, with a genuine look of concern. "This is pretty far out west. Are you sure you have the right place?"

"Of course, I do. We wanted something different. You know, for a special memory," Cara explained.

"Well, it'll be different, that's for sure." The driver frowned and drove forward.

When they finally arrived, the taxi pulled right in front of the bright red door of a small clapboard shanty painted the ghastliest yellow with a rusty bell hanging lopsided on the roof. There was nothing else in sight, but an old jalopy parked to the side. "Perfect!" Cara exclaimed, while Carl and Rusty stood outside the car, mouths ajar, alarmed by what they were seeing.

Cara walked around to the taxi driver's window, leaned in, and whispered, "Stay, please, this will only take a few minutes." She handed him a fifty-dollar bill and winked with one eye and then the other, not having ever before winked at anyone or even practiced winking in front of the mirror.

The six steps up to the freshly painted red door were narrow, flimsy, and lacking handrails. The three of them had to hold on to each other to keep from falling off. Cara could tell that Rusty disapproved of her choice, but she knew that he wouldn't complain, being only a few minutes away from inheriting half her fortune. As for Carl, he was simply flabbergasted.

"Come in!" a raspy, but strong voice bellowed. "Ah, the bride and groom have arrived." When the old man smiled, a glob of wet tobacco gathered at the corner of his mouth. "And you brought a witness, too. I'm so glad because my wife died two days ago, and she usually fills that role."

"Oh, I'm so sorry," they all three spoke at once.

"Not to worry. She was ready to go, and at least she finished painting the front door." He offered his outstretched hand to welcome the groom.

When he reached for Carl's hand, Carl ignored him and quickly turned to study the old photograph hanging on the pink cracked stucco walls. "Is that her?" he asked, pointing to the plain woman, her face badly sagging, sitting next to a younger version of the Justice of the Peace standing before them.

"Yep, that's Clarise. God bless her pretty soul. Now, are you ready? We're having the funeral here shortly after your wedding, so we best be getting on with the ceremony."

Determined to see it through Cara bit her tongue to keep from doubling over with laughter when she spotted the wife's casket standing up in the corner, a tattered handmade quilt draped over it, her name embroidered in the center.

"Well, I can say this, Cara," Rusty said, offering a feeble smile, "we won't forget *this* wedding...*ever*. Matter of fact, we probably should keep it our little secret. Don't you think, Carl?"

Carl manically shook his head up and down and fought back the tears.

Cara gave Rusty a severe look. "Let's do it!"

They turned to face the old magistrate, who had been standing quietly holding the Bible, waiting for the couple to come to their senses. He pushed the button on the old cassette player with his nicotine-stained finger and "Going to the Chapel of Love" poured out from its tiny speaker. As if on cue, he raised his voice and began the ceremony with "We are gathered here today...."

Cara looked over at Rusty, who was staring ahead at something way beyond the old man, either at his future or at the cockroach clinging to the wall. Carl openly wept behind them, issuing apologies in between tissue blows.

Just before the Justice of the Peace came to the "I do" part, Cara stopped him. "Rusty," she said, turning his direction. Rusty, still staring ahead didn't respond. "Rusty!" she yelled.

"Oh, what?" He shook his head and rapidly blinked his eyes as if to wake up.

"Before we sanctify our marriage, I need to tell you something." She raised her voice and belted out, "I'm gay!"

The old man shuffled backwards out of harm's way and knocked over the cassette player. Carl gulped and swallowed a gasp. Rusty stood perfectly still and straight-faced.

"OK," he said nonchalantly, looking over at Carl, trying not to smile. "I think we can live with that."

"And..." Cara drew out the word as if waiting for a drumroll, "and my grandmother has taken away my inheritance."

That bit of news did not wear well on Rusty or Carl. With tightened lips the look on their faces resembled George Costanza on *Seinfeld* right after one of his crazy schemes foiled.

Cara clinched her hands tightly on her hips and leaned forward just inches from Rusty's face, now drained of all color. "You are supposed to say, I think we can live with that, too."

Rusty's eyes grew wider and when Carl began uncontrollable whimpering, Cara turned toward him, thrust her hand down his shirt and pulled fiercely on his necklace. His body fell forward when the chain didn't release. Dropping to his knees he croaked, "You're choking me, you're choking me!" Cara pressed her knee into his back and forcefully yanked until the clasp gave way and broke just when Carl threw up. Rusty, never having seen Cara so violent or Carl vomit, had fallen backwards in sheer horror. The old magistrate simply clutched his Bible to his chest, and looking over at the casket in the corner, he said, "Do you see what I'm seeing, Clarise?"

Looking like a crazed woman, Cara slung back the hair that had now fallen in her face, kissed the Irish ring, and threw the chain at Carl. She turned to the old man and said, "Keep the forty-five dollars, your honor, and marry these two!" Then she jerked the engagement ring from her finger, tucked it into Carl's front shirt pocket, and ran out of the chapel. Before she slammed the door, she yelled, "Don't get too excited about that ring, Carl. The jeweler said it's a twenty-nine-ninety-five Cubic Zirconia!"

"But wait, Cara, where's the hotel...how do we get home?" Rusty yelled, lunging after her, only to trip over a cane that had been conveniently placed there by the smiling JP.

Back in the taxi, Cara yelled to the driver, "Step on it!" Through the trail of dust (taxi drivers love the speedy getaway and will peel out any chance they get) Cara looked back and saw Rusty rushing out of the chapel. Carl, just seconds behind, crashed into him, and sent them both flying off the rickety stairs to the gravel driveway below. She sighed heavily and slumped down in the seat.

When they were far enough away, and she had the taxi driver in stiches after telling him the entire story, she called her sister. "Hi, Brynn. It's done. I left them at the chapel. I'm on my way."

"Good! Looking forward to hearing all about it. I'm in the hotel bar. There are lots of gorgeous men here."

"Yeah, well don't devour them all. Save one for me," Cara said fretfully, imagining all the men in the bar sitting around her sexy sister while she sat all alone sulking. Determined to end the petty jealousy, she came clean, hopefully for the last time. "Listen, one more thing, Brynn…it was me that tore off your Barbie dolls heads and buried them under the sandbox. And I was the one that told dad you backed into the garbage cans. And while I'm at it, remember that stain on your prom gown?"

"I know. I know, Cara. I already knew most of that stuff. You've been confessing all week. Enough already!"

"You knew?"

"Of course, I knew. The whole family knew. We just hoped you would grow out of it. And you did."

Before Cara realized that Brynn had hung up, she said in the softest most sincere voice, "I hope so. But what I've been really trying to say, is…I'm sorry, sis."

A tear rolled down her cheek, and when she looked up, she saw in the rearview mirror, the taxi driver watching her dewy-eyed behind John Lennon wire-rimmed glasses.

When she wiped away the tear, she noticed red paint smudges on her fingertips. "Oh no, I guess that painted door wasn't dry yet." She showed her hand to the driver and the laughter started up again.

Leaning over the seat, she tapped the nice man on the

shoulder and handed him a peanut butter cookie. "I always carry cookies with me. I made these myself," she said with a proud grin.

"My favorite! Thank you! You're Cara, I know. I'm Ivan."

"Hey, Ivan, want to join me for drinks at a fancy hotel bar? My rich and gorgeous sister's paying."

"Sounds nice," he replied. Flashing his teeth, he switched off the mileage counter. "Care to join me in the front seat?"

Cara noticed that he was wearing braces, and that made her feel right as rain. "Yeah, I'd like that."

"No, don't pull over!" she cried out when he let his foot off the accelerator. "I've never climbed over a front seat before. I think it's time I tried it."

"Be my guest."

Slipping the Irish Claddagh ring back on her finger, Cara made sure the heart was facing outward, open to love.

WHAT SHE DOES BEST

"$\mathcal{W}$hat do you do best?" he asked, nodding her direction.

She thought long and hard. Let me see...at $75 an hour, that's $1.25 a minute, about $5.65 worth of wasted time I'm spending right now looking for the answer to that question. So, here's my best guess. "Nothing, really," Heather answered, forcing herself not to roll her eyes.

"Surely there's *something* you do best. Come on, think about it a bit more. It'll come to you," the therapist urged, tapping his pencil on the notebook resting on his groin, his legs tightly crossed, sitting erect in a tall shiny gray leather chair that his client imagined he spent hours mulling over in the store where they sell fancy chairs to professionals who need to look virtuous while making a living sitting down.

"Well, everyone likes my Apple Swirl with the Girls cake. Can that be what I do best? It's not an easy cake to make."

"Seriously."

I bet he practiced that frown, too, Heather thought,

trying not to be mean, but it wasn't her idea to share her personal shit with a stranger.

"OK, write. I like to write, but is it truly my best? Thought provoking, romantic, cute, all those things, but my best? If it were the best I could do, I guess I wouldn't need a dictionary, a thesaurus, a book of idioms, Wikipedia…"

Heather shifted uncomfortably in her chair. "OK, OK! Loan officer, five years' worth. But I'm without any clients, not even a referral. So, I'm working a second job now. Loans can't possibly be what I do best…not anymore."

"Am I a good listener?" she repeated his question. "Mostly, but sometimes while I'm listening, I picture myself doing something else, like cleaning the keys on my computer, or slapping the person in front of me who's yammering on and on. And sometimes I come up with great ideas while listening, and sometimes I nod off, but I prefer to call it short little energy naps."

Silence.

"Sometimes I'm good at being funny. Do you think that was funny what I just said about listening?"

More silence, except for the tapping on the notebook from the man in the shiny shoes looking dubiously at her. He allowed enough seconds to pass for her to notice a subtle glow emitting from a dozen or so gold framed credentials on the wall behind him. The dimmed gold leaf and crystal lamps positioned evenly on each side framed the group perfectly. *Nice touch, King Midas.*

The therapist cleared his throat in an effort to bring her back to the question at hand.

"Yes, I suppose I am avoiding the question. I don't have all that much to say, but when I do, it comes out in long drawn-out sentences that even confuse me. It's as if I'm having a conversation with myself in the end... kind of like right now."

Heather frowned, looked at her watch, and tapped it with her finger repeatedly. "Hey, maybe I'm best at knowing when to *quit*."

"Yes, you're right about that," the therapist said dryly. "See you next week, same time?"

"No, I don't think so. I don't think this is what I do best, but tell my mother thank you for the therapy session."

Later Heather thought more about the question. She called her ex-boyfriend. "You know, we were together for a year, and you probably know me more than anyone. So, could you tell me what you think I do best?"

"Oh, that's easy. Love. You do *love* best."

"Then why aren't we still together?" she said almost in a whisper, almost afraid of his answer.

"Because that's not what *I* do best."

"Oh. Thanks for taking my call," Heather said blandly. "Goodnight." She hung up the phone in a hurry before Dean could hear the quivering in her voice. His answer was clear as a bell, unusually poignant for a man who was not the sharpest tool in the shed. But he was her first love, and that counted for something.

She turned the lamp off, tucked a throw pillow between her legs and slept through the night on the sofa that she and Dean had bought together a year earlier. It still smelled like pizza.

The next morning, she awoke to a *knock, knock* on the door. Groggy, a crick in her neck, thinking she might have been dreaming, she sat up and listened. The knock came again, this time with five melodic bangs and a follow up ending with two more. If her brother had not been out of town, she would have thought it was him.

"Who is it?"

"Special Delivery!" a male's voice announced.

"Oh, uh, OK, well, just a minute, please. Uh, do I need to sign, or can you just leave it at the door?"

"I'll leave it. No problem, lady. But don't forget it's out here!"

"Ugh!" Heather caught a glimpse of her crumpled face in the mirror, as she stood there counting seconds before opening the door.

"Forty-nine, fifty!" she stated and stuck her head out into the damp empty hall. Scanning the floor, she saw a beautiful bouquet of flowers in a most unusual vase.

"Oh my, flowers," she hummed, gently placing the bouquet on the small kitchen table that also served as her desk. The vase was the color of the most brilliant purple, and a beautiful "H" was etched vertically on one side, filled with what looked like molten gold. "H for Heather. Awww."

The flowers were wild with colors that screamed "happy," and she couldn't help but giggle. She searched all over for a card, but there was nothing. Checking the hallway to see if it had fallen out, she again found nothing. She shrugged her shoulders and began preparing a hearty Saturday morning breakfast.

With coffee brewing and toast crisping, she couldn't help but look back at the flowers often, nor could she stop the perpetual smile smeared across her face. It had been a long time since she had been given flowers, much less smiled. She had been such a sad sack since her break-up with Dean, how could anyone find her attractive? And surely, they weren't from *him*. The big oaf never gave her anything. She took an unusually long time eating as she pondered who could have been so nice to her at a time when she could really use some kindness.

It was a good day to clean out the closets, suck up the cobwebs from behind the furniture, and wipe down the dusty fan blades that she would have never noticed if her mother had not pointed them out. While living with Dean, she had succumbed to a slovenly lifestyle, as his bad habits were so engrained, he was simply untrainable. With the music on, she had her apartment spic and span in no time. She had forgotten how nice it was to have a neat and orderly place, and the flowers looked even more beautiful on a clean, polished table. "I have a secret admirer," she cooed.

Monday morning, she had just stepped out of the shower when another unexpected knock on the door came loud and clear.

"Who is it?" she yelled standing in the hallway, wet hair dripping down her back.

"Special Delivery!" a muffled voice announced.

"I, well, can you leave it there, please?"

"Yes, but don't forget it's out here!"

"I won't. Thank you!" Heather rushed back to the bathroom and wrapped her hair in a towel. Quite anxious to see what could possibly be at her front door, she nearly tripped over the lumped up braided rug in the hall. Nearsighted since she was ten, and nearly blind without her glasses, it took her a good three minutes to find them.

Hoping no one was nearby, as she was wrapped in her favorite tattered robe that she had to retrieve from the garbage pail the last time her mother had visited, she cautiously opened the door. Quite perplexed, she stared down at a box wrapped in white paper, a deep red velvety ribbon tied around it.

"Oh my," she sang, her eyes wide with pleasure as she placed it next to the flowers. No note was attached to it, no writing on the paper, no company name or logo.

She poured a cup of coffee, sat down and slowly untied the ribbon. The gift was about the weight of a box of candy, and she expected to find just that inside. Instead, she found a handsomely carved wood jewelry box; on top the letter "T" was filled with rhinestones. "My last name...Tate," she beamed.

Heather felt as light as a feather on her way to work. The fine feeling was still with her as she walked into the department store and took her place behind the counter where she began organizing the fragrances of the day.

"Wow, what happened over *your* weekend?" Charlene, her friend and co-worker leaned on the display case all ears. "You're absolutely aglow. Dean change his mind?"

Heather's smile dropped. "No, there's no chance of that."

"Well then...tell, tell!"

"Yes, do tell," Theodore's head popped up next to Charlene's elbow.

"Oh!" Heather jerked back, still not quite used to Theodore's presence. He was the only markedly small person she had ever known, and his head was the size of an average man, so when he appeared suddenly like that, just a view of his face from the neck up peering over the glass counter, she couldn't help but be a bit startled. And to top it off, he always looked at her with the irresistible eyes of a Labrador puppy; soft and brown, hopeful. Unnerving, yet charming, the little guy always made her smile.

"Just having a good day, that's all." Heather sprayed a sample of her favorite perfume on Theodore's hand. "What do you think?"

"Nice. *Very* nice."

"Theodore, you should buy some for your girlfriend," Charlene teased. "But it *is* expensive."

"Hmm, good idea. Wrap one up for me," he said.

"Lucky girl," Heather teased when she handed him the perfume. He did a little jig as they watched him walk back to his office, hopping on the escalator to the second floor.

"Does he *have* a girlfriend?" Heather asked Charlene.

"Anything's possible. That sure would be interesting to see. I wonder if she's a little person, too." Charlene snatched up the sampler perfume bottle. "I need a squirt. There's a good looker over there in women's underwear. Maybe this will get his attention. See you later."

Even Theodore has a girlfriend, Heather thought, suddenly feeling sorry for herself. And look at Charlene with all that optimism. The good feelings she had earlier blew right out the department store electronic door. They returned later when she saw Dean having lunch just a few buildings down from her workplace. But they quickly left again when the cute brunette, she had seen him with before, joined him. Avoiding them both, she skipped lunch, and found herself sulking behind the counter, sitting on the floor dusting the store merchandise.

That evening when she arrived at her apartment, an ordinary brown envelope was sitting on the door mat. It was addressed to her with no return address. She was disappointed not to find another gift. Still, her smile returned when she walked in to see the flowers and the jewelry box waiting for her on the table. She'd open the envelope later.

A pot pie, a sitcom, and a quick phone chat with her brother, Heather was about to call it a night when she remembered the envelope. Probably something from the landlord, she surmised.

She carefully opened it, as she always did with her mail, and pulled out a thick greeting card. From the seemingly ordinary card popped up a 3D version of a very cute dancing elf kicking his legs up with a big grin on his face, arms open wide as if asking for a hug. The letter E was printed in bold red on his pointy green hat. She had always loved elves, but who would know that besides her mother? She sat it next to the jewelry box and instead of sleeping on the sofa, she felt like sleeping in her own bed.

HH

The next day, back at the perfume counter, Theodore came by to visit, as he often did. "Would you like to have lunch with me today?"

Caught off guard, Heather looked around for Charlene; nowhere to be seen. They had gone to lunch many times together, but never alone. "Oh, I, well, I actually brought my lunch today. But thank you," Heather lied. Why she told such a fib, she wasn't sure. She was fond of this man. He was always so nice to her and Charlene. An odd feeling came over her.

"I can grab a sandwich next door and join you. Where do you eat when you bring your own?"

"I, uh, I sometimes sit in my car and listen to NPR. I doubt you'd like that very much," she frowned.

"Oh no, I love NPR. I'll be back in a few, and we'll walk out together."

Before she could protest, he darted off. She watched his thick black wavy hair move swiftly past the stretches of countertops, past the women's dresses and disappear around the corner. Ten minutes later he was back with a paper bag and two bottles of water.

"Theodore, I guess I forgot my lunch," she said meekly, searching the shelves for a lunch that didn't exist. "It's not here. Raincheck?"

"Aww, don't worry. I have an extra-large sandwich we can share. Allzeit bereit!"

Heather's brow furrowed, "What?"

"Scout motto, be prepared. I was a scout until I was eighteen. Guess it stuck." His wink and smile were so engaging, Heather could not conjure up any more excuses and found herself sitting in the front seat of her car with a charming, four-foot-tall Boy Scout sharing a foot-long hero sandwich.

On the radio, they listened to a segment about, of all things, love, and the different kinds and levels. Heather wanted to ask Theodore about his girlfriend after she had shared the details of her break-up with Dean, but he jumped out of the car before she could say more.

He politely opened her door for her. "My lady," he bowed.

"Thank you. I really enjoyed our conversation," she heard herself say with a small chuckle. "And thank you for lunch."

The little guy stepped up on his toes and opened his arms wide. A hug was anticipated. Heather bent down, and just when she put her arms around him, someone spoke from behind. "Guess you're not moving on to *bigger and better* things, I see," Dean said with a sneer. His brash voice boomed inside the confines of the parking garage concrete walls as he walked pass them.

Heather watched him move across the parking lot with a noticeably haughty stride, and before Dean turned the corner, he gave her a silly finger wiggle wave. Realizing she had been fixated on Dean, she looked down at Theodore and he was gone. She didn't see him the rest of the day. She would have to wait to apologize.

When she arrived at her apartment, yet another box was on her doorstep. The excitement from before wasn't there. This time she left the box on the table while she showered and slipped into her pajamas. She fixed a bowl of ice cream and plopped down in front of a chick flick. She didn't want to think about the special lunch with Theodore, the hug interrupted by Dean's rotten remark, and the crummy feeling she had watching him walk away, and then Theodore leaving without a word. And the lie. Why did she have to lie?

The movie over, the ice cream melted in the bowl and a pile of used tear-stained tissues by her side, Heather decided she would open the box in the morning when she was certain she'd be in a better mood. She curled up on the sofa and eventually fell asleep; this time ignoring the book on being single that her mother had given her, lying face down on the coffee table. The cover showing beautiful thin women skipping down the street all smiles and happy with their single selves was not something she wanted to look at. Even though her mother meant well – she always did, she would remind herself – Heather hoped she wouldn't be giving her a pop quiz on the book anytime soon.

The perfect sunny morning woke Heather up to the weekend. The coffee pot brewing always made her feel hopeful. A cinnamon roll drenched in butter helped wipe away any rotten remains from the day before. She was now ready to open the box. What was revealed inside took her by surprise. A bottle of "O", her favorite perfume. "Mom! This must be from mom. She knows I love this stuff."

After skimming through the single's guide, just in case any unexpected questions were tossed at her, Heather made a phone call to her mother. The conversation went as usual and not without another light scolding for refusing to schedule a second appointment with the therapist, upstaged by a descriptive article on ankle-slitting stalkers hiding underneath cars parked at the mall, and soon Heather was back to square one with guessing who the secret admirer might be. She placed the perfume next to the elf and stood back looking at the four items, the morning sun shining behind them from the kitchen window. Then it struck her that she should take a picture. Maybe Charlene or even Theodore could help her solve this mystery on Monday. At least it would give her an excuse to have lunch with Theodore again, and to apologize. She snapped a picture with her cell phone and looked for other things to do to consume her thoughts.

Not wanting to be late, Heather hurriedly dressed for work, and while on the way out the door her phone rang.

"Hey, hey, hey," Dean's familiar greeting made Heather stop in her tracks.

"What do you want, Dean?" she said sternly.

"If you're not having lunch with the dwarf today, think we could meet up?"

"That's not very nice. I wish you wouldn't say that. He's a friend of mine and yesterday…"

"I know, I know, but come on, *you* and that runt? You've got to be kidding! But honestly, I need to talk to you about something kind of important. Lunch at our favorite restaurant by your work?"

"Well, I was going…." Wanting to steer clear of any more of Dean's crude remarks, Heather stopped herself from telling him that she was hoping to have lunch with Theodore. Then it occurred to her. Could Dean be her secret admirer after all? Was he jealous?

She agreed to meet him.

Theodore was at her counter when she arrived. He was sitting on the stool set up for the shoppers. When she approached him from behind the counter, he was eye level. Expecting a glum face, he carried the sweetest smile and for a moment, his size had not occurred to her at all.

"I'm sorry I took off without saying goodbye yesterday," he offered before she could apologize first.

"You took the words right out of my mouth," she said, dropping her chin to her chest. "I actually brought you a sandwich for a peace offering."

"Excellent! We can finish off the rest of that segment on NPR," he flashed a grin. "I've got some interesting thoughts on the subject."

"That's what I had in mind, but my, well, my ex-boyfriend wants to meet me for lunch. Says it's important."

"Oh?" Theodore looked down with tightened lips as if to stop himself from saying something. It didn't help. "Why would you do that?" he asked, looking into her eyes with a genuine concern. "I mean, he dumped you, didn't he?"

"Yes. Yes, he did, but you see, I've been getting these gifts since then from someone anonymous, and it could be him. He's never given me intimate gifts like these. It's as if he knows me now."

Theodore let out a puff of air. "He's not a nice guy, you know. Are you sure it was him?"

"No, but there's no one else it could be. So, I have to find out."

"Find out WHAT?" Charlene moved into the conversation with the ease of a cat, but as loud as a parrot.

"I'll catch you ladies later," Theodore said, hopping off the stool with a graceful agility. He gave them a quick wave over his shoulder.

"But, what about your sandwich!" Heather yelled, waving at Theo with a smile that triggered a curious look from Charlene. Heather ignored her and began skimming through the photos for the picture on her cell phone that she took of the gifts.

"Charlene, I have a secret admirer. Look at what he's sent me this week."

"Nice stuff!" she ogled. "How do you know it's a *he* that's sending you gifts? Ever seen Shanna in Men's Apparel? She looks at me like she wants to dress me up in a pair of Italian pleated pants."

"Yikes! She doesn't look at me at all. Guess I'm not her type." Heather crinkled her nose. "I think it's Dean sending these things. I'm going to find out at lunch today."

"Excuse me, miss, if I can take you away from your *friend* during work hours, I would like a sample of each of those perfumes," a stout, well-dressed lady pointed with a fingernail as long as an anteater's. "All nine of them."

"Good luck, girlfriend!" Charlene said backing away. "Can't even imagine Dean being capable of that kind of romance, but stranger things have happened. Shoot, even Theodore has a girlfriend! Ha, ha, ha!"

Heather gave Charlene a scowl that switched to a fake smile when she turned to assist the boorish customer.

Noon arrived and Heather's associate, who was coming to hold down the counter, was a few minutes late. Heather nearly ran out of the store to the restaurant where she breathlessly searched all around for Dean. When she couldn't find him, she sat at a small table in the corner and waited. Twenty minutes had passed when he finally walked in. He spotted her and headed her direction.

Plopping down on the chair, apparently a man on a mission, drink orders were taken, and both were quiet until Dean spoke. "I think I owe you an apology."

"Well, yes, twenty minutes is a long time to keep someone waiting," she stated with arms tightly crossed.

"No, not that...for breaking up with you the way I did. I was told that a text is not the right way to end a relationship. So, here I am, apologizing."

"Thank you," was all Heather could muster up.

"Friends?" Dean held out his hand.

"Hmm." At first, she hesitated, then she let him shake her hand. *Gee, why does he have to be so cute.* "Uh, Dean, as a part of your apology, did you by chance...well, here let me show you." She handed him the cell phone. He squinted curiously at the picture of the gifts, and at that precise moment the brunette who she had seen him with twice, tapped him on the shoulder.

"Oh, you made it." Dean looked up at her with a big smile. He leaned over and patted the chair next to him for her to sit down. "Heather, this is Diedre," he stated as casually as if it had been planned, and apparently it had.

Heather merely nodded. Her lips felt perfectly numb, no words on her tongue.

"Hi," Diedre said and turned her attention to the phone in Dean's hand. "What are you looking at?"

Dean faced the picture Diedre's direction. "I'm not sure, looks like somebody's birthday gifts. Was it *your* birthday?" he asked Heather with a dumber than dumber look.

"Next month, Dean, next month," Heather sighed heavily, now knowing the gifts were definitely not from him. *The big dummy couldn't remember my birthday even if it was a label on his favorite beer can.*

"Oh, how nice," Diedre said. "Must be from someone special. That's some expensive perfume. And the letters…hmm, let me guess. I play a lot of word scramble games. This one is easy. See the H on the jewelry box, the T on the vase, the O on the perfume and the E on the card? Shuffle them around and you get…Theo! How clever." She looked up at Heather, all radiant. "Is that your new boyfriend Dean was telling me about?"

"What?" Heather grabbed the phone from the unwanted guest, removed her glasses, and held the picture up to the light. "Oh, my goodness, it sure does."

"Theo, who's Theo? Oh, let me guess," Dean sneered, "your midget man?"

"Dean! Stop that! Just why did you ask me here? And what do *you*, have to do with this meeting?" She glared at Diedre.

"Well," Dean reached over for Diedre's arm and explained, "I thought you'd want to know that Die and I are moving in together." The gooey smiles passing between them made Heather's eyebrows twitch.

"Why would I want to know that?" Heather's condescending voice wiped the smiles right off their faces.

"Well, truth is, we don't have much furniture and that sofa we bought together is technically half mine, and the refrigerator I loaded up and carried *all* the way from your mother's house, well, technically…"

Heather put her hands over her mouth, either to keep from saying something terrible or to stop herself from screaming. Either way, she couldn't believe what was happening. How shallow, how rotten these two were in front of her, and how could she have even allowed herself for one second to believe that Dean had any feelings left for her. She was mortified.

"Aw, Heather," Dean softened his voice, "remember, the best thing you do is *love*. So, give us a little love here. We really need it," pleading now with his hands. "And honestly, we could use some pots and pans too."

Heather glanced down at the photo staring up at her. The letters gleamed underneath the light from the hanging lamp. THEO. Why hadn't she seen that before? She looked at Diedre differently now. She could see that she was dreamy eyed over Dean, just like she had been at one time. So open to love was this young woman that she was able to see Theo's name in the letters, when she had not.

In the awkward silence, with her newfound awareness and the couple looking at her like children waiting for their allowance, she felt her heart soften, her shoulders drop, and she didn't know why, but she wanted to cry. Someone approached their table just in time to stop her from making a fool of herself.

"Hi, Heather."

She recognized the voice, slapped her glasses back on, turned the phone facedown, and looked over to see standing before them, bigger than life, Theodore. Darling Theodore saving the day!

Heather caught an ugly look in Dean's eyes, and before he could say something offensive, she grabbed Theodore's hand and rose from the chair. "Theo, meet Dean and Diedre. I know, I know, I'm late for our lunch date." She bent down and kissed Theodore on the cheek. "Isn't he the sweetest?" she said to Diedre, ignoring Dean altogether.

Diedre clasped her hands together in prayer and smiled starry-eyed, as if she were blessing them.

Dean started to say something, but Heather stuffed a napkin in his opened mouth and spoke for him. "Yes, of course, you can have the sofa *and* the refrigerator."

"Aaa sum pos ah pahs?" Dean said, grabbing her by the arm as she turned to walk away.

"OK, and some pots and pans."

He spit out the napkin from his mouth, and yelled, "What about the crockpot?"

"Give it to him, Heather," Theodore said, challenging her with a sensible countenance. "Maybe your secret admirer will give you a new one."

Heather yelled back at the couple, their necks eagerly stretching up like baby birds waiting for a worm, "It's all yours!"

Out in the parking lot, they feasted on sandwiches while listening to NPR in her car. Heather thanked Theodore for the timely rescue. After that, neither said another word about the embarrassing situation in the restaurant, and to her surprise, she didn't reveal that she knew his secret.

There was a loud knock on the window that startled them both. Dean pressed his nose against the glass on Heather's side. She rolled her eyes at seeing his smashed face.

"What now?" she moaned and lowered the window. Theodore sat up taller.

"You know, I was right," Dean said, shaking his head a little too excessively, apparently nervous about what he was about to say, "you do *love* best. I just wanted to tell you that I admire that."

"Thank you, Dean. I appreciate that. And?" She suspected he had more to say and didn't just pop up in the garage to talk about her attributes.

"And…since you do it so well…" he paused, inhaling deeply, a painful look appearing on his reddened face.

"Save your breath, Dean. You can have the exercise bike."

"YES!" he held up his fist victoriously, as Heather rolled up the window before he could ask for more.

"And hey, little dude, be nice to my old girlfriend," they heard him yell as he slapped the hood of the car on his way back inside.

Without further interruptions, they finished off the segment and their sandwiches in silence.

❈

Heather never had the chance again to let Theodore know she knew he was her secret admirer. No more gifts appeared at her doorstep, nor did Theodore come by her counter to visit. A valuable opportunity had been missed and she blamed herself.

Soon after, Charlene met a man in the lingerie department and quit her job to travel with him. Heather came home from work every day since heavy hearted.

Another week passed and Dean and Deidre picked up the things Heather had promised them and left her with a bean bag in return. She told them the good news that she had landed a job with a successful mortgage company. They congratulated her and simultaneously asked for the coffee pot.

On the last day of her perfume sales position, she went upstairs to Theodore's office and was told he had moved on to another job. She felt just awful losing a boyfriend and two friends in such a short period. In her sadness, she went out to buy new furnishings.

It was raining outside on the morning of Heather's birthday when a knock was heard at her door. "I hope that's not my new sofa and refrigerator in the pouring rain!"

She yelled, "Who is it?" as she yanked on the zipper of a pair of jeans.

"I have a delivery."

"Oh no!" she grumbled, slipping into a t-shirt. When she reached the door, the delivery men weren't there. She sighed with relief and before closing the door, she spotted a box on the floor.

"Ohhh," she giggled, and although it was kind of heavy, she carried it as if it were a carton of eggs. She placed it on the table, sat down in front of it, and stared at it. On the side of the box, a happy birthday sentiment was written in red.

The handwriting was unfamiliar. Timidly, she took her sweet time to open it.

"A crockpot?" she said out loud. Closing her eyes, a familiar face emerged from falling glitter beneath her eyelids, and the scene in the restaurant with Dean and Deidre appeared. "Maybe your secret admirer will buy you a new one," his voice was heard through the sparkling rain.

Another knock, a soft thumping of the knuckles disrupted her pleasant thoughts. Heather wiped away a tear and went to welcome the delivery crew.

Grabbing some plastic bags, she opened the door, prepared to protect the flooring from their wet shoes. She quickly gave her instructions. "Please be careful of the..."

But not a soul was there to receive them. "Oh!" When she scoped the ground for another possible package, something popped out in front of her.

"Oh!" she said again, this time stepping back from the threshold. Upon seeing her friend standing there, within seconds, a warm smile moved easily across her startled face. "It's you."

"Happy Birthday," Theodore sang, looking up at her with those warm puppy-dog eyes, his arms wide open, stretching up from his tiptoes like the elf in the card. He wore a red ribbon around his neck and an amazing smile that only a secret admirer could have for a girl who knew exactly what she did best, but just needed a little reminder.

On Tap

BAR PEOPLE

*A*s a fiction writer, many of my story ideas are derived from the people I meet at restaurant bars and pubs. To remember them, I secretly sketch them with my fancy stylus pen on my cell phone app. I am not, by any means, an artist, and that is why these drawings are so raw and sometimes a little weird. (Let's not forget there also may be a little wine involved.)

The range of personalities I mingle with are all over the map. These wonderful, interesting, and innocent people spark my imagination without even knowing it. Most of them become endearing to me, as do all the characters I write about. So, here's to the bar people you are about to meet! Someday all the drinks will be on me. Cheers!

JOSH

*B*ehind the bar and take-out.

Neat guy. Personal. A little angry. Just enough to make him sexy. He wore the coolest shirts and one with the number 69 written all over it. That was a conversation that lasted about ten seconds too long. Phew! Come to find out this young man was in love with a woman that he was afraid to approach. Of course, yours truly offered to help him with that.

He likes old movies, the black and white gooey love stories. So, I suggested he invite her over for one of those corny flicks, and since he loves to cook, make her something culinarily desir-able, non-gaseous, of course, and since he loves wine, be sure and bring out the best. And if *she* doesn't like wine, cancel the dinner. Never trust anyone who doesn't like wine. Oh wait, I have a lot of beer drinker friends, so scratch that remark. Otherwise, Josh got the best

of my semi-worldly wisdom. But later, when I went back to find out how it went on his quest for love, he was gone. Kaput! When I asked the staff if anyone knew what happened to him, they said, "Josh? There was no Josh that worked here."

MARY

a regular at the bar with the kindest eyes and smile. She likes everyone, and everyone likes her. Next to her sits her husband, a handsome man with a big grin staring ahead in wonder.

She explains it to me, as I watch him walk away, his leg dragging behind his step and his arm held in a 'hand on the steering wheel' position. She tells me he had a stroke several years back and that he's not the man he used to be. He used to ride a motorcycle, was a natural gardener, welded sculptures for a living, and made love to her like no  man ever could. But no matter what, she still loves him and will never abandon him, even when he gets angry and throws things at her. She knows that he loves her, too, and deep down inside he so much misses the man he used to be, and she will never stop looking for that man in his eyes.

DURSTON

He didn't like me when I first met him. He watched me warily from his shifty eye, always facing forward, like a gunslinger just waiting for a barfight. Well, I couldn't have that! I sensed that there was a sweetheart behind that rough exterior in the faded Grateful Dead t-shirt hanging loosely over a substantial belly, and the long silvery- gray ponytail that looked as if it had not been released from the rubber band by him or anyone else for quite some time. He had great legs, and no wonder, he worked for UPS – in and out of those brown delivery trucks, day after day for thirty years. Wow, have you ever seen a UPS driver in those cute brown shorts with those good-looking legs? I have.

He's retired now and living a life of ease, single, happy, worriless, fishing, camping, and lots of music festivals. I thanked him for his dedication to getting those all-important packages to us, rain, sleet, or hail…no snow, after all this is Texas. He hasn't given me the evil eye since. I would venture to say, he likes me now. Here's to the UPS! Clink!

MICHAEL AND KELLY

*V*alets of the sweetest kind. They don't even give me a claim ticket, and sometimes they park my simple little green Subaru in pole position where normally a hot BMW owned by that sexy friend of mine usually gets first dibs.

I probably remind them of an old aunt that used to bring them presents from NYC or San Francisco, some place young people think is cool. I bring them cookies from home or food from the restaurant. College kids are always hungry, sick of dry noodles, and for them to be working so hard at this thankless job, I knew that was the nicest gift I could give them, besides a warm hug. Someone suggested that a bigger tip might have been a better idea. Hmm, I'm not so sure about that.

JORGE

A very cool dude. He's from Nicaragua
and wore a t-shirt with one big word on
it – *Immigrant.* And of course, that is a
huge topic these days. Our conversation lasted an hour with barely any
pauses in between and lots of intensity.
He is in the middle of a divorce, sadly.
And most sadly because he has three
children under twelve. He showed me

their pictures, and I just had to ask him if there was any way
he could repair the marriage – for the sake of the family. He
said his wife had fallen in love with someone else and is
wanting to re-marry. I searched and searched my heart to
find something to say that could help him win her back. But
that word LOVE, that powerful, unbridled, hypnotic word is
as unshakable as Kryptonite, and all I could do was drop my
head in a quiet surrender to his demise.

So, we talked about cigars instead, which had the disappointed women next to him moving down a seat. He promised to share some of his premium beauties with me someday. Although, I knew in my heart, that "someday" rarely happens.

BOLIVER

A tender of the bar but not of his patrons – cold, uncaring, ignoring me and my friends, not interested in impressing us at all. Makes a helluva mixed drink! I liked this bar, great happy hour, so I had to do something to change the sour attitude of this Peter O'Toole lookalike and quickly. Sitting there alone one night, I asked him, "What will it take for you to be *my* bartender?" He responded with ease, "Well, I brought you a glass of water, didn't I?" I laughed, he didn't. He was serious.

I can't resist a challenge, so I asked him about himself. "My father deserted us when I was a teen after he burned down our house and blamed it on me," he said. "If that's not enough, I was named after Boliver Shagnasty, a character on the Red Skelton sitcom. And my brother is suing me for stealing his comic books. And I'm saving up for earlobe surgery after removing one-inch flesh tunnels.

"See…" He pulled off his cap and flicked at his earlobes with a finger. A mass of dangling loose flesh jiggled, as he slyly moved the tip jar closer to me. I winced and dropped him a ten.

No wonder the poor guy is so miserable. I gladly passed the hat at the bar for his much-needed surgery. No one should have to go through life looking like Dumbo. Even if it's their own fault.

BOB?

He gave me several names to choose from. One was a french name, but I couldn't pronounce it properly, and I didn't want to butcher it like Texans do their cattle, so I just settled with Bob. I was in a weird mood when we met, so I figured I could easily handle this unusual and interesting man with an impish grin. I might have been wrong.  He eyed me like a taxidermist sizing me up for a mounting. In between political outbursts, he softened and at one point, when talking about how much he admired his wife, I spotted a tear in his eye. Then he turned into a standup comic, and before I knew it, he had me laughing my head off. I was having a great time until without warning, he started talking about male body parts, and that's when I decided to give up my seat to the impatient woman eavesdropping behind me trying desperately to order a beer. Seems she liked talking about male genitalia, too, and soon they were laughing it up like locker room buddies. He even bought her a drink!

But not one for me. I guess I didn't have the balls.

BUTTERCUP

Bar floor waitress engaged to the sweetest and shyest waiter. They met at work, bumping, and squeezing past each other between tables of obnoxious patrons with their glasses tipped high. He called her Buttercup. She swooned when he said it. I watched them fall in love, move in together, and fret over meeting each other's parents. Once  wide-eyed, nervous, and twitterpated, they are now like an old married couple, relaxed and smiling at one another as if they were the only two people in the room. See, true love is the greatest thing in the world, I told everyone in the place.

I dropped in several weeks later and saw the shy waiter, but no happy waitress, Buttercup. He came over wearing a frown and said that she had quit and moved on to another job. I comforted him with a squeeze of his arm. When he turned to walk away, he looked back over his shoulder and said through clenched teeth, "We broke up! I hate her!"

I went home early that evening feeling sad. I cuddled up with a bowl of Ben and Jerry's and watched *The Princess Bride* to keep from crying and losing my faith in true love.

MR. MANAGER

Nicest guy ever – wears classic-fit suits
and lively ties and has the face and
sparse mustache of a budding teenager.
He doesn't flirt, or look you up and
down, or touch you like he's your
friend, or show eagerness to be
acknowledged. He treats everyone the
same. His expression is like a child's
simple, "Won't you be my neighbor"
look.

He makes you feel welcome even though you've done
nothing to deserve it. Why is he so nice when you can't even
remember his name? He has an unadulterated essence about
him that makes you wonder if he even really exists. His face
will show up in your dreams, or in a crowd, or on the inter-
net, and you will still not remember his name. But you *will*
remember *him*. Funny how that works.

DOREESE

Bartender, for a while. She appeared one day with arms a flappin' like a city pigeon that never flies, just ruffles its feathers and hops like it's about to take flight but never does. Her Bronx accent was loud and abrasive, and spit gathered around her mouth when she was yammering on and on about something nonsensical. She said with emphasis, "I have no stinkin' desire to stay at this gin joint another week," and *poof* she was gone. She went on to law school, and I bet you in a few years, we'll see this strong-willed, ambitious, animated woman representing people in high places, like that guy everyone knows by his orange hair.

MICHELLE

The bar belle with killer curls that I would have died for if only the product she used to keep those curls silky and curly hadn't been such a secret. I thought I was negotiating with my old Aunt Lorraine who refused to give up her cinnamon bun recipe for fear that she'd lose the best thing men liked about her...her buns. I made a fool out of myself begging her.

One day by pure accident I ran into Michelle in the restroom. She was standing in front of the mirror scratching her partially bald head and holding her curls in her hand. A wig? She's wearing a wig! I was speechless, and so was she. We stood there staring at one another, on the brink of tears. And when women know that words are not enough to express what they feel, they simply hug. So, we did.

MR. THOMAS ANONYMOUS

The annoying guy at the bar. There's always one. He's a close talker, so close you can tell within seconds what he had for dinner and what he's about to drink. I admit, I tried to like him, even after all the women warned me. But he is who he is and has been for his fifty-two years on this planet…annoying!

We've got the women who hog the chair next to them with their purses that look like glorified bowling ball bags, the seat hoverer trying to get you to guzzle your drink so you'll leave and give up your stool, the inappropriate toucher, the loud cell phone talker, the guy who reads an entire novel and orders only iced tea, the woman who has a tasting of ten different wines before choosing, and then there's our one and only, Mr. Anonymous. We call him Thomas, only because it rhymes.

TYLER

Cutest valet in love with the cutest waitress. This kid is so cool. I enjoyed chatting with him out in the parking lot on those wispy Fall evenings. He's smart, witty, charming, and struggling through his senior year in college. His future plans are to be a politician and marry Maggie, buy a house, get a dog, a ski boat, and a room just for his  books. He's worried about the entitlement he sees oozing from his generation and how easily it is to become lazy and give up. He will make a difference. I'm looking forward to seeing him on television, in the newspaper, and on the ballot someday, because this honest, hardworking, respectful, and kind young man is just what our country needs.

BARTENDERS

*S**cooter*** - a bartender with braces, who is dating ***Candie*** - a bartender with a most voluminous derrière, who is having an affair with ***BJ*** - a bartender who wants a divorce from his mousy wife ***Rebecca*** - a sweet and shy bar manager in her innocent glasses and tight bun who would never hurt a fly.

Bartenders now behind bars, they got caught serving underaged patrons, over-serving, drinking on the job, and diluting the vodka. It went off the rails when some creepy bar friends revealed that BJ was having an affair with Candie. And being so enlightened, sweet Rebecca ripped off her glasses and let down her bun and started a barfight scene that is still talked about to this day.

BJ got the divorce he wished for, but when Scooter got his braces off, Candie fell in love with him again and left BJ in the dust with a broken heart and a broken nose. Rebecca skipped bail and ran off to South America with her attorney.

MS. ANONYMOUS

She was seen at the bar each time with a different man. Only the bartenders knew what was going on, and their tips counted on their utmost secrecy. But they confessed that they never knew her name because the men always paid for her drinks and paid in cash. Except one time, Doreese, whose life was shortened as a bartender, heard the name Sybil,  and since she was leaving for good, why should she care if we knew. So, now we know this woman with a long list of men is Sybil, but we regulars just call her Kibble. That way, everyone's safe.

ERIC

A five-foot-two bar patron who drives a
one-ton pickup and likes to be called
Stud. He speaks Arabic and says he's
from the Middle East. We heard
Thomas Anonymous, on his third Pina
Colada, ask him if he eats camels in his
country. We moved about three seats
down from this guy who never ceases to
annoy us. Last we heard, Eric opened a

new restaurant called "Hooves" and yep, you guessed it, the
main entrée is Kamel Kabobs, and in the winter, Kamel
Stew. And the funny thing is, Thomas Anonymous is his
partner.

RICK

The guy with the best pick-up line I've ever heard at a bar. "Don't you remember me? I was the trumpet player on the hit song, "I'm a Girl Watcher," and he proceeds to sing it and sound out his trumpet part. Well, if that doesn't count for a free drink, I don't know what does. But then he kept singing it and tried to get everyone within earshot to sing along. I'll buy you *three* drinks if you stop singing right now! That darn song stayed in my head for five whole days!

I'm a girl watcher
I'm a girl watcher
Here comes one now
Toot ta toot toot ta toot toot!

I bet it stays in your head, too.

A QUIET STRANGER

A lovely man, kept his head down as if in prayer, a pen in his hand, no paper. Like an unlit cigarette being held out of habit – a habit he wished to kick. "Draw me something," I boldly said, placing a napkin in front of him. With barely a glance, he effortlessly sketched and held it up with a faint smile. A view from his fantasy window. Ahh! May I have it, please? He slid it down the bar. I bought him a drink and politely left him – a lovely man, alone with his zen, quietly stroking his pen.

HIM

He's a sweetie pie. The guy I like sitting next to when I'm not hunting for more writing material. People say he looks like John Lennon. Others say, Dustin Hoffman. He has the profile of Ben Franklin. His big brown eyes and fabulous sense of humor make me forget all about my Stylus pen and my bar friends and that we're sitting only one  seat down from the fabulous Matthew McConaughey.

$\mathcal{A}$nd who says all you do at the bar is drink? I have a whole new appreciation for the bar, lounge, tavern, pub, dive, saloon and their staff and guests. And all I had to do is show a little compassion and thoughtfully listen to these ordinary people with their interesting life stories. You should try it sometime. You may be pleasantly surprised by what you hear. Hold on, someone's tapping me on the shoulder.

"Excuse me, I don't mean to bother you while you're in such a deep discussion with yourself, but is this seat saved?"

"Of course…just for *you*."

HOCUS POCUS

Devil's in my closet
Trying on my girlfriend's shoes
Says she wants to go dancing
Shake me from these blues
She's telling me it's time to leave
Stop watching the six o'clock news!
I turn the volume up
And focus on you

Devil's in the front seat
Telling me how to drive my car
Hiking up her skirt
She thinks we're going far
She's begging me to find neon lights
And stop at the nearest bar
I turn down the witchy woman song
And focus on you

Focus, focus, focus on you
That's all I ever really wanted to do
Hocus Pocus she wants to cast her spell
The devil's trying desperately
to take me down to hell

Devil's sitting next to me
Made me buy her a drink
I see her in my reflection
Stop talking, I'm trying to think!
Now she's kissing me behind the ear

I'm trying not to sink
I raise my hand for another round
And focus on...on...on...

Devil's in the back seat
I think she's really drunk
Should have left her at the bar
Or stuffed her in my trunk
A cop pulls me over
He takes the devil off my hands
Says we're going where we can do no harm
But officer, you don't understand!

Focus, focus, focus on you
That's all I ever really needed to do
Hocus Pocus she tried to cast her spell
But I'm safe behind these bars, babe
and she's going back to hell

FORBIDDEN

---

*N*early two years held hostage in his parent's home, Hardy sat on the window seat lethargically gazing out across the yard watching the new neighbors move in. His eyes brightened when he saw the girl. Tall and lanky, she wore all black. Black t-shirt, black shorts, black shiny leather motorcycle boots. Her long unnaturally blue-black hair was thin and straight with spiky bangs pointing downward on her forehead. She reminded him of Lydia from the movie *Beetlejuice*. He'd know that face anywhere after watching the movie at least a dozen times with his parents who still cherished the film since its birth in the late eighties. Lame! With only one television in the house, the choice was always theirs. If it weren't for his mother's home-made brownies…

Hiding out from the dreaded Corona Virus, Covid-19, SARS, whatever the hell you call it, and now its evil offspring Omicron, had taken its toll on the sixteen-year-old. Because his mother was immunocompromised, abnormal precautions were taken, forcing a wedge between him and his friends.

"Don't let those filthy beasts near your mother!" his dad demanded. Talking on the phone was boring. It always had been. School sessions on Zoom made him sleepy. The same video games, the same movies, all-night Monopoly, and the dictators forcing a thousand-piece jigsaw puzzle on him was enough to make Hardy feel like an irritable old codger. Codger, one of the many words he had learned from his father who often spouted their meanings from the dictionary he kept in the side pocket of his recliner. Even the smell of popcorn in all its glorified butter was no longer exciting. Tiring of it all, everything began to look old, even the dog.

There were times during those long days of captivity when Hardy found himself soaking in the bathtub plotting his parent's slow, tortuous death. Through the air vent, he listened to them tinkering in the kitchen discussing the next meal and arguing whether or not an eggplant was a vegetable, fruit, or a "they." His dad would win the argument, of course, as he was the only one with a college education, he often reminded her. His mother worked from home coding health insurance, while his father worked in a chemical lab conducting experiments. Their humdrum talks over dinner, amplified by their irresponsible opinions stemming from the Fox TV channel drove Hardy up the wall. Often, he'd wear earplugs under his long unruly hair to keep from hearing them argue.

Then it happened. 2022! On the night of the dullest New Year's Eve party imaginable with only his fully vaccinated aunt and uncle present, a big turkey dinner with all the trimmings was worshiped and consumed in the dining room. After stuffing themselves, followed by a game of dominoes and three rounds of Uno, Hardy watched the adults slowly drift into a tryptophan coma, spiked eggnog in fancy glasses resting on their bellies while watching *When Harry Met Sally*.

He could have set the house on fire, and they wouldn't have noticed. Entertaining that thought almost made the evening worthwhile.

Cherry pie was served just minutes before midnight when his parents proudly announced over champagne that they were returning to the real world. Masked, of course. But nevertheless, rejoining the humans. Then his father sheepishly added that his mother would be moving out and living with her terminally ill sister. A sacrifice made for the whole, when in truth, they were formally separating. Covid had taken its ugly toll on them, too. Hardy was relieved that now he didn't have to dirty his hands with murder.

Instead of feeling bad about his parent's pending divorce, Hardy could barely sleep that night thinking about his freedom. He would, of course, elect to live at home with his poor suffering father who would no doubt take on extra hours in the science lab to soothe his broken heart. The world that had become unreal and distant was now at his fingertips.

Drawn back to the window, Hardy said excitedly, "Time to escape!" Emboldened by watching the maskless girl carrying boxes one by one into her home, he decided it was a good day to make a new friend. He ran past his mother robotically vacuuming the carpet while listening to an audiobook on her oversized old fashioned pink headphones. She looked up and yelled, "Haircut at three o'clock!"

He managed to dodge his father bent over the sink, fixing a faucet leak. "I could use your help, son…" his words were chopped off when Hardy slammed the back door. "Where's your mask, young man?" he yelled, bumping his bald head on the faucet.

Her name was Felicia. She was different. Seventeen and bold, and unlike any girl he'd ever met, she liked to explore.

For some reason far beyond reason, he wanted to kiss the black lipstick off her sensually plump lower lip.

They set off maskless on their bicycles on a gray Saturday morning. Neither had their driver's license; the pandemic being his excuse; something she'd rather not talk about, was hers. The air was thick with moisture, not a cloud in the sky, just a dreary blanket of dirty haze hanging above them. The same way it had felt inside his home, he told Felicia.

After a three-mile ride, they stopped in front of an old, abandoned clinic – the windows barred up with wood, the overgrown weed-filled grass carrying a rusty *Do Not Trespass* sign. They walked around it slowly, studying the weather-beaten façade. At the back of the building, a door was left ajar. Felicia slowly opened it and poked her head inside. "Come on, let's go in," she giggled, stepping confidently over the warped threshold.

"Are you sure?" Hardy questioned, looking all around to see if someone was watching.

"Come on, I've been in here before. Plus, I've got a flashlight."

When did she have a flashlight? He hadn't seen it in her hand.

Inside, the building smelled weird – a strange mixture of mold and alcohol and something putrid no one should ever learn how to describe. They rounded the corner, and all went pitch black. No longer were they comforted by the dull light emitting from the back door exit. Felicia pointed the flashlight up and down the hallway – along each side at least a dozen doors. She opened the first one.

"This is the head nurse's office. She was not a pleasant woman."

"How do you know?" Hardy asked.

"I told you, I've been in here before."

She moved on to the door across from it and pushed it open so hard, it bounced off the wall. Hardy jumped. Felicia turned toward him and placed her hand softly on his beating heart while she shone the flashlight underneath her chin. Her lips and her eyes disappeared in the dark, leaving only her flat white face glowing disturbingly close to his. She looked deliciously wicked. It felt like the ideal time to kiss her lipstick off, until she backed away from the perfect moment and said, "It's OK, it's just the inoculation room. *So* many needles."

Feeling silly cowering behind her, Hardy moved ahead to the next door. He placed his hand on its surface and hesitantly stood before it.

"Don't go in there!" Felicia yelled.

"What do you mean?"

"I said, don't go in there. It's forbidden. It's locked and for a good reason."

"I wonder why," he snickered. His natural curiosity made him reach for the door handle. "It locks from the outside. Strange."

"People were tortured in there. Screaming was heard for hours." Felicia directed the light to the floor. "See, there's blood seeping out from underneath the door. You're even standing in it!" She pointed the light to his hand still clasped to the doorknob. "And look, now it's on your hand! Come on!"

Hardy wiped his hand on the grimy wall and followed, relying on her flashlight to lead the way. She walked slowly, unafraid, and purposely down the hallway.

A door creaked open from behind.

"What was that?" Hardy whispered hoarsely, grabbing Felicia's hand.

"Who cares? Let's get out of here!" she screamed, jerking her hand from his bloody grip. Hardy fumbled along after her.

Whoomph!

He fell flat on his face from tripping over something in the dark. "Felicia, wait!" The light from the flashlight disappeared around the corner.

He tried to get up, but something had a hold of his leg. He pulled, and it wouldn't let go. Sitting up, he reached down in the blackness and felt a hand, boney knuckles in loose crusty dry skin wrapped tightly around his ankle. No arm attached to it. Just a hand. He kicked and kicked, and attempted to pry it loose, but it wouldn't let go. Then he tried to stand.

Whoomph!

Down again, his body tumbled backwards, and the loud crack that was heard was his head banging the tile floor.

In a foggy consciousness, he felt the hand drag him through the sticky blood and into the forbidden room. "Mom! Dad!" His silent scream ricocheted off the walls of his skull and rattled around in his head as his forehead slammed into the door casing.

From the other side of the closed door, he heard Felicia's faint nervous laughter.

And then the click of a lock.

ENSNAREMENT

The bold Italian has landed on you
Her thick tongue and muddy eyes have you hypnotized
She weaves glitter and gold about your head
And becomes the man while in your bed

Tightening the noose around your neck
She will shamelessly bring you to your knees
Soon you will be her better man
Perhaps you should run while you still can.

THROUGH THE FENCE

*O*ut of the blue, like a child throwing a sudden temper tantrum, the wind made a huge fuss on a very calm November evening, and as quickly as it came, it left. *Weren't you supposed to be here in March?* Grace silently argued with nature, sitting outside alone on the deck watching her boyfriend flipping through a magazine while nursing a beer at the kitchen bar on a Friday night when most Millennials who cohabit usually went bar hopping, stumbling home after midnight, eager to make love with what little energy they had left.

"Do you have something you want to say to me?" he had said earlier, standing at the end of the hall, far enough away to create an echo for dramatic effect.

"Except that you're acting weird?" she retorted, mirroring him with her stance, waiting to see who would back down first.

As it had been for a while now, they had nothing else to say, and it seemed another weekend was going down the tubes. Grace went straight to the kitchen and selected a large red goblet from her collection of mismatched glasses. Slowly fuming, she stood in front of the shelf full of wine and ran her fingers over the beautiful labels, some dusty, too young to open, and at the top, a new case of Old Vine Red that was turned on its side for easy access. For now, her sour mood called for a less expensive bottle, so she snatched one from the box.

Gil kept his eyes glued to the article he was reading, as she poured herself a glass and clumped past him, making an unpleasant sound with her plastic slip-on shoes that drug across the fake wood flooring on her way back outside to talk to the only one that would listen – the man in the moon.

Grace slumped down into the hammock chair trying to get comfortable and within reach of the table that held her favorite beverage. The quick gusts of wind earlier had left an eerie silence, and from beyond the wooden fence she could hear the neighbors next door stepping out onto their porch.

"I am sick and tired of your nonsense!" the female voice spoke, followed by the sound of a metal chair being drug across the cement.

"Must you sit so close, Mindy?" the male voice asked.

"Unless you want the whole stinking neighborhood to hear us!" she said, dragging the chair back across the concrete.

Grace didn't move – finding interest in the couple's conversation that was way too familiar. She let her wine sit idly by while she waited for one of them to speak again.

"Look," the woman began, "I really don't know *what* you're thinking, but how am I to know if you won't talk?"

"There's nothing to talk about, and besides, you wouldn't listen anyway," he said, in a weary tone.

Grace heard a "humph!" from the female, followed by a

slamming of a door, and then a car screeching out of the driveway.

"Give me a break!" he grumbled.

"I know just how you feel," Grace said, having a sudden sensation of déjà vu. "Sorry for eavesdropping, Mark, but you guys aren't exactly the soft-spoken type."

"Oh, hi Grace. I'm glad it's you, I thought I was hearing voices," he said, chuckling into his glass. "What are you doing sitting all alone in the dark?"

"I thought it was safer out here until I heard you guys. Ha!" she scoffed, sitting up to take a sip, but first looking down into the glass to make sure that bugs weren't swimming in it, like they did the last time she sat out on the deck licking her wounds.

"Yeah, well, it hasn't been exactly ideal around here lately." He put his feet up on the ottoman and sunk deep into the seat cushion. "Not sure if it can be fixed," he sighed, a tinge of sadness in his voice.

"Must be in the air. Seems like things are kind of unraveling around here, too." Then Grace blurted, "I think my boyfriend's having an affair." And as quickly as she said it, she wanted to take it back.

"Oh, man," the neighbor winced.

"I'm sorry. I shouldn't have said that … it's just that, well, I need to talk to someone or…."

"I completely understand," Mark groaned. "Hey, I don't want to add to your mess, but since we're sharing…I think my girlfriend's trying to get me to end our relationship."

Just then, Gil opened the back door and said facetiously, "Are you talking to yourself again?"

Grace calmly responded, "Nah, just talking to the man in the moon. He likes to listen, and actually cares."

Mark squelched a laugh, biting down hard on his bottom lip.

"Great, well, I'm sure the neighbors would appreciate it if you two would wrap it up my midnight. Kevin just called and asked me to meet him for a beer."

"That's nice. The Grand Cru is still in at Doc's. It's really tasty, and they're running a three-dollar special tonight," Grace offered, knowing with Gil's frugal nature, he couldn't resist the opportunity.

"Sounds like a plan, thanks. I'd invite you, but I know how much you loathe Kevin." Before he shut the back door, he added, "Not sure when I'll be back, so leave the porch light on."

"I will," Grace said to a closed door. "You, big lug!"

"Thanks for not exposing me," Mark began, after he heard Gil's car drive away.

"Not certain what good *that* would do," Grace groaned. "He'd probably claim that *we* were up to something sneaky. He's been insinuating that I'm having an affair all week long,"

"Oh, I know that one *really* well. Mindy's been saying weird stuff like that to me, too. Shoot, if I were having an affair, would I be sitting on my back porch on a perfectly good Friday night talking to the fence?"

"Wait just a darn minute!" Grace protested. "So, I'm a fence, am I?"

"No, no, not at all," he said apologetically. "Even though I've only known you a few months, the conversations we've had have been really enjoyable."

"I agree. Thank you. We had a nice chat at that party awhile back, too. That was interesting that Gil and Mindy knew the same people."

"I know. I was really surprised to see you there and actually glad. I didn't know a soul in the room. Did you?"

"No, not one. Gil said he'd played tennis with the guy who threw the party. I just came along for the fun of it."

"Hmm, Mindy said she played tennis with the guy's wife. Small world." Mark paused to take another drink. "Well, I did notice that you two left early."

"Yeah, Gil wanted to go to the gym. He said he had to work out some kinks in his neck. Thank goodness for twenty-four-hour gyms. Not for me, though. I went straight to bed."

"Come to think of it, ever since we went to that party, Mindy's been acting strange," Mark said, starting up the uncomfortable topic again. "I confess I got a little drunk, but nothing out of the ordinary…not enough to *leave* me there to find my own ride home. And to top it off, she didn't show up here until after two. We've been fighting ever since."

"That's crummy. Gil's been acting odd himself. Three times this week he's hung up the phone quickly when I entered the room, and when I confronted him, he said I was crazy and probably feeling guilty from my own indiscretions." She paused, shaking her head, "That's just plain ludicrous."

Mark cleared his throat, "I've heard about this kind of reverse psychology before from a friend who recently divorced. He said it went on for almost a year. The silly fights over nothing almost drove him crazy, until finally his wife spilled her guts and admitted to an affair. He said he was almost relieved to end the nonsense."

"Hmm, I won't put up with this nonsense for *that* long."

"Can you hold that thought for a minute? I could use a refill." Mark stood up, waiting for an answer.

"Good idea, I could use…well anyway, meet you back here in five." Grace grabbed her glass and went back inside.

She bypassed the kitchen and went straight for the bathroom. When she looked in the mirror, she scolded her reflection. *Oh, your hair looks terrible! The ponytail has to go!* She ripped the hair tie off and shook loose the tight curls. *What the hell am I doing? He can't even see me.* Still, she felt better after a dab of lipstick and a quick brush of mascara. And for some reason, she had the sudden need to shed the baggy gray t-shirt and slip into a pretty flowered blouse.

Forgetting all about the wine, she peeked through the side window to see if she could somehow spot Mark on his porch. The fence was too tall and the ivy that had covered it for years had piled high enough to give the neighbors even more privacy. Grace laughed at herself and went back outside empty-handed.

"I'm baaaaaack," she sang in a sweet singsong.

The two neighbors, relaxed in their seats, bantered back and forth through the fence before continuing the serious discussion they had abandoned during their break.

"You know," Mark said, "while you were inside, I was thinking about what we were talking about earlier, and I know guys are considered obtuse, but I really do think that Mindy's trying to tell me something."

"I suppose," Grace paused, bearing in mind that the weightiness of the subject might require a helpful answer. "I think… if you know someone's behavior well enough, you can tell when something's not right. Like, I know when Gil is upset about something before he even tells me. His pattern changes. It probably helps that I'm naturally intuitive. Maybe you are, too."

"Hmm," Mark said, followed by silence, as they both contemplated her words.

"It's not fun to think about, is it?" he finally spoke.

"No, it isn't!" Grace stood up so quickly, the swing chain

rattled when her feet hit the deck. "This is silly, us sitting out here on a fabulous Friday night while our so-called mates are out having a good time."

Mark leaned in. "Where are you going?"

"I think I'll mosey on over to Docs. A cold beer suddenly sounds good. Interested in joining me?" Grace asked, peering through a crack in the fence.

"Well, I'm not about to pass up moseying. My car or yours?"

"Yours would suit me just fine."

※

The parking lot at Doc's was spilling over with cars, and Mark had to park two blocks away. As they approached the bar from the rear, Grace spotted Gil's orange Ranger in the very back of the establishment. She almost didn't see it – partially hidden behind a tree. She mentally notated that in her newly suspicious mind.

"Boy, the beer drinkers are sure out tonight. Look, even the outside area is packed." Mark pointed to the crowd. "Think we can get waited on?"

"Tell you what," Grace suggested, "why don't you go inside and get us a Grand Cru before they're all gone, and I'll save these last two seats for us." She hurried over to claim them.

"Good idea. Be back in a few."

Grace watched Mark nudge through a cluster of bikers and when he slipped through the back door, she immediately scanned the area for any signs of Gil or Kevin. Curiosity got the best of her, and she couldn't stop herself from going over to Gil's truck to look inside. His windows were heavily tinted, so she had to press her nose against the glass and cup her eyes from the tree lights overhead in order to see. Everything looked like Gil inside — his stained Texas Tech coffee cup, a clipboard, gym bag and papers thrown from the front seat to the back — except for the blue cashmere sweater she spotted on the passenger's seat. She turned quickly, thinking she might be seen peering into a vehicle that wasn't hers and walked back to the empty chairs.

Mark came out just when she sat down and handed her a beer in a frosty mug. "Did you by any chance see Gil inside?" she asked nonchalantly.

"No, I wasn't looking for him. Besides, it was too crowded in there, and there's another band inside and a lot of people were dancing."

Grace was certain he caught the concern in her eyes and looked away. She toyed with the idea of telling Mark about the sweater in Gil's truck, but suddenly she felt ashamed that she was spying on her boyfriend. She decided not to mention it.

The Elvis cover band had finished their break and resumed, playing one of Grace's favorite songs. She got lost in the lyrics and sang softly along. She hadn't noticed the couple walking behind them until she looked back as they walked away. They were arm in arm and giggling while they stumbled to their car. Grace recognized the man — the back of his head was one that she had shaved many times, and the expensive Italian shirt that she had given him on his birthday was splotched with sweat that didn't seem to bother the female who was clinging to him.

"Don't look now, but …," she nodded her head toward the couple.

Mark looked over, squinting his eyes in disbelief. He slowly rose from the chair. "Is that *Mindy*?"

Grace quickly grabbed his arm. "Mark, please sit

down," she pleaded, gently pulling him toward her. "I'm sorry, but it looks like we've been duped. That's Gil she's with."

"What?" he asked, looking back and forth from Grace to the couple. "Oh man, you're right."

Grace sighed and let go of his sleeve. "You know, I've often wondered how I'd behave in a situation like this. But my instincts tell me to sit tight and do nothing just yet. Does that seem right to you?"

"If you're worried that I'll do something stupid, like break your boyfriend's nose, or cause a scene yelling at Mindy, I can pretty much promise you that's not my style. Sure, this bothers me, but since she's with Gill, I kind of feel responsible for your feelings, too. Make sense?" Seeing that she was forcing back tears, Mark reached over and placed his arm round Grace.

"Makes a lot of sense. I was actually thinking the same thing about you." Touched by his kindness, she rested her head on his arm.

Not able to resist, they both turned and watched the couple, now getting into the back seat of Gil's Ranger. Stunned, Grace looked wide-eyed at Mark, and mouthed in a hushed tone, "Oh my *God!*" All of a sudden, the whole scene became funny, and they started nervously giggling, hunkering down in their chairs, shoulder to shoulder, Grace covering her mouth to keep from being heard.

"Please tell me you're thinking what I'm thinking," she said between gasps and titters.

"Yes, but let's let them get comfortable first," he winked and elbowed her in the side kiddingly.

The two conspirators sat motionless, closely watching the orange truck, doing their best to keep their imaginations intact. Ten minutes felt like twenty, and when the band finished playing another tune, *It's Now or Never*, Grace stood up and said, "It's now or never!"

Mark led the way, while Grace hung on to his elbow from behind. When they reached the truck, the windows were completely fogged up. Their whispers to one another could hardly be heard under the sound of the band's poor version of *Jail House Rock*, so they slipped behind a nearby tree to discuss their next move.

Grace had an idea that sounded great in her head, but ridiculous when she said it out loud. "Let's just bang on the back window and hide and see what they do."

"You bang, and I'll open the back door and scare the hell out of them," Mark whispered in nervous excitement.

"Do you really want that visual in your head for the rest of your life? With those heated up windows, they've got to be doing more than just kissing." As tempted as she was to shock Gil, she suddenly felt silly. She could tell that Mark was feeling uncomfortable, too, by the way he was tugging at his moustache.

Just then, two policemen pulled up on motorcycles. Removing their helmets, they were clearly on duty; guns dangling, and boots polished. Grace came out from behind the tree and walked toward them. Mark followed her obediently.

"Sir," she said ever so politely, "I mean, sirs."

Robotically, the two uniformed men turned around at the same time. "Yes ma'am," the taller of the two said with a distinct East Texas twang, slowly tipping his head, his lips held tightly together.

"I was wondering. I think there's a couple of teens making out in the back seat of that truck," she turned and pointed, "and I don't know if you have kids or not, but I bet their parents wouldn't want them to be doing that. Do you think maybe you should sort of scare them a bit and teach them a lesson?" Grace lifted her eyebrows, anticipating a laugh from the officers.

Both men peered over at the truck, looking for signs of lewd and lascivious behavior. "Yep, it looks like something's fogging up those windows," the shorter cop said, frowning up at his partner who was seriously eyeballing the situation.

"Thank you for your concern, ma'am. We'll handle it." The cops walked directly up to the truck, one on each side and knocked on the doors, peering through the windows with their flashlights. The truck shook as the alarmed occupants fumbled nervously in the back seat. You could hear from inside, "Shit, shit, shit!" and "Hurry up!" and Grace later said she thought she heard, "Take my darn bra off your head!" Of course, the story would get even more exciting the more it was told.

Mark and Grace stayed hidden while watching the scene, as the crowd hushed and the musicians stopped playing, all eyes turned toward the orange Ranger. When Gil and Mindy finally got out of the truck, they stood with heads down like two caught children, while the short policeman scolded them, and his partner looked disconcertingly down at the ground. Grace noticed that Gil had on only one shoe. For a split second, she felt sorry for her humiliated boyfriend, but that feeling was quickly replaced with disgust. She turned briskly and walked away. Mark followed.

"Hey there," Mark casually said, slipping his arm around Grace's waist. "I'm hungry. Want to get a bite to eat?"

"Well, I suppose I could eat something," Grace answered, a little startled by his cool manner, but appreciating it all the same. A thought sent a mischievous little smile to her lips. She stopped and faced Mark. "Think we should invite Gil and Mindy?"

"Why not?" Mark shrugged and looked back at the couple. Mindy's eyes followed his. "I bet they're hungry after exerting all that energy. Shoot, when was the last time you made out in the back seat of a vehicle?"

Grace burst out laughing.

"Oops, looks like they spotted us," Mark said. "Now we'll *have* to invite them."

The mortified looks on their faces was almost too painful to watch. Mark gave the guilty pair a curt nod and turned to Grace all smiles. "Heck, I bet they'll even pay for it. What do *you* think?"

"I think they already have."

ROUGH AROUND THE EDGES

Can't take her to a restaurant
Can't leave her at the bar
the girl's making me crazy
sometimes she goes too far

Always talks in the movies
keeps a beer in the bottom of her purse
my friends think I've gone bonkers
for a girl that drives a purple painted hearse

Cracks her knuckles in the middle of church
sings along when she shouldn't sing along
In her hair she wears a plastic daisy
Beneath her skirt, a crocheted thong

Cooks me bacon on the engine of her car
Only dances when the music's turned off
They all wonder why I keep her around
She's my 67' Chevy, a Rachmaninoff

So what she's rough around the edges
So what she's one of a kind
So what she likes to give me wedgies
The girl's not perfect, by she's all mine

LOOK BACK

I had more to say
when you turned and walked away
I needed for you to look back
I stood there staring
thinking you were caring
and certain that you would look back
You walked past the park
through the tunnel dark
and still, you didn't look back
Over the bridge
along the river's ridge
till you faded and wouldn't look back
I stayed for awhile
waiting for your smile
imagining your arms opened wide
I'd meet you halfway
and you'd breathlessly say
I promise to stay by your side
I thought I had more to say
the day I walked away
and decided to never look back

NEVER AGAIN

*S*he just couldn't stop thinking about it. Everywhere she looked she was reminded. It stuck to her brain like a big bug smashed on the windshield of a car. She saw it in the bushes, on a carton of milk, on the bottom of her shoe, and in the reflection of the librarian's glasses as she scanned her stack of books. It left her briefly when she swerved to keep from running over a nervous squirrel that couldn't make up its mind which way to go; her car ending up on the sidewalk where she sat in a daze, feeling ridiculous that she could have been killed by a fat rat with a cute, furry tail. On her tombstone, "Death by Squirrel," flashed before her eyes. She laughed hysterically. But even in that moment of hilarity, she saw it again in the rearview mirror.

Driving ever so slowly – "like an old lady!" a red-faced teenager yelled at her while screeching past her car – she finally made it home safely. She ordered pizza for dinner to avoid finding it in the refrigerator. And for a split second, she considered inviting the scrawny, pimply delivery boy in to help take her mind off it. A couple of gin and tonics on the back porch only enhanced it. It followed her to bed, up the shadowy stairs and into her bedroom behind the lampshade. It even sneaked inside the Bible she read every night before retiring. She avoided the bathroom altogether until the last minute. Forget taking a shower! No way!

The night would be a long one.

"Never again, never again!" she scolded herself while lying in bed hiding under a blanket, still dressed in her clothes, including her running shoes. Just in case.

She hid there until the perspiration stung her eyes, and the rancid pepperoni breath forced her to come up for air. She turned on classical music hoping to drown it. Then back under the covers she went. The more fatigued she became, the closer it got until she could no longer hold her eyes open another second.

As she drifted off, it started to fade until she felt herself being sucked into a storm drain. NO! The sudden jolt forced her eyes open – falling, jerking, falling, jerking, again and again until finally surrendering to pure exhaustion. *

"ZZZZzzzzz."

From somewhere above the dark surroundings, she heard a familiar whisper, "Honey, honey, it's me, I'm home." Her husband stood over her and slowly removed the blanket from his wife's face.

Her eyes popped open in sheer terror. She shot straight up from her catatonic stupor and let out a hair-raising scream that forced her husband to jump back from the bed. And yes, as it was designed to do, the horrible sound from her crookedly stretched mouth did indeed cause the hair to rise on the back of his neck.

"Good heavens, what's the matter? he demanded, hoping her head wouldn't start spinning next.

"Oh baby, I'm so glad you're back! It's been awful, just

awful!" She reached out with both hands and pulled him into her shaking, wet body, her fingers clawing at his love handles.

He spoke into her damp disheveled hair, smelling oddly like stale popcorn. "Do I need to take you to the hospital, call the police, what is it?"

"Never again! I promise!" she snorted into his chest, vigorously rubbing nasal mucous on his heavily starched dress shirt. "Never again!"

Gently pulling her head back, the husband studied his wife's blotchy, sweaty face, and madly twitching eyelids. He reluctantly asked, "What did you *do?*"

"I...I...I went to the movies," she choked on her words, and the frightened expression suddenly switched to an angry one. "Your crazy sister made me go. I told you she hates me. It's all *her* fault."

Then in a snap her face fell flat, and she held a disconcertingly haunted stare as if she had been hypnotized. He lightly shook her from her trance. "AND?"

She spoke timidly, as if confessing to a crime, "I saw a movie."

"AND...what was *it?*"

"Yes, exactly," she whispered, her eyes darting past him.

"What?" The husband shook his head, more confused than ever. He followed her gaze over his shoulder. He saw nothing out of the ordinary. Emphasizing each word slowly and precisely, he tried repeating the question. "What – is – it – you – are – trying – to – tell – me?"

"I can't say..."

"You can't say *what?*" he asked, raising his voice.

"I can't say..." she whimpered, her eyes widening again. She pointed to the wall with a trembling finger. Her head began to shake violently, and in a bloodcurdling scream she cried out, "**IT!**"

Rearing back, the husband stared helplessly at his crazed wife freaking out over a stupid wicker laundry basket standing against the wall.

In a sudden wild move, the wife sprung off the bed, ran screaming from the room, down the stairs, out the front door, and into the dark rainy night.

"What in the hell is IT?" he yelled at the top of his lungs.

The poor frazzled husband stood there in a cloud of uncertainty as a red balloon floated past him and out the door.

The end.

*I've always wondered what that gap between falling asleep and jerking back to reality is called. Hypnagogic jerk. Cool, huh?

By the way, "it" is written in this story 26 times.

⊞⊞

Here is an alternative ending for the Baby Boomers:

Gently pulling her head back, the husband studied his wife's blotchy, sweaty face, and madly twitching eyelids. He reluctantly asked, "What did you *do*?"

"I...I...I went to the movies," she choked on her words, and the frightened expression suddenly switched to an angry one. "Your crazy sister made me go. I told you she hates me. It's all *her* fault."

Then in a snap her face fell flat, and she held a disconcertingly haunted stare as if she had been hypnotized. He lightly shook her from her trance. "AND?"

She spoke timidly, as if confessing to a crime, "I saw a movie."

"AND...what was it?"

"Si...si...." she whispered, her eyes darting past him.

"What?" The husband shook his head, more confused than ever. He followed her gaze over his shoulder. He saw nothing out of the ordinary. Emphasizing each word slowly and precisely, he tried repeating the question. "What – is – it – you – are – trying – to – tell – me?"

"I can't say..."

"You can't say *what?*" he asked, raising his voice.

"I can't say..." she whimpered, her eyes widening again. She pointed to the bathroom door with a trembling finger. Her head began to shake violently, and in a bloodcurdling scream she cried out, "Psycho!"

Rearing back, the husband covered his ears and stared helplessly at the crazed woman now up on her knees. He'd had enough of her nonsense and decided to play along.

In a sudden wild move, she sprung off the bed. He grabbed her by the arm and held her tightly to his chest. "I know what you need, baby." He lifted his eyebrows flirtatiously, accompanied by a sinister smile. "You need a long, leisurely shower. I'll take one with you. What'd you say?"

The wife jerked from his arms and ran hysterically screaming from the room, down the stairs, out the front door, and into the dark rainy night.

The poor frazzled husband pulled off his tie, let out a small chuckle and proceeded to take a shower. Walking toward the bathroom door, he stopped in his tracks when he heard the shower curtain closing; the rings loudly scraping across the metal rod.

He stepped softly into the bathroom. Spotting the plunger sitting by the toilet, he reached for it, held it in batting position and ripped open the shower curtain. What he saw caused him to drop the plunger and fall back against the sink.

There stood his sister, a bloody rubber knife in both hands held high over her head with a deranged, wild-eyed look on her face that he remembered seeing often as a child.

Her maniacal expression quickly broke into an innocent wide-mouthed grin, and when she burst out laughing, she fell back against the tiled shower wall and comically slipped down, landing on her bottom. As usual, her crazy antics had her brother instantly doubling over in an unrestrained belly-laugh.

Outside, while running in circles around the house, the wife stood in the rain incensed by the raucous laughter coming from the bathroom window. What she did next, one can only imagine.

The end, again.

VANITY

Where does she go from here?
Her body gets fuller from year to year
The face peels, the eye lifts, the expensive wine
Under low lit candles, my she looks fine

Her reflection refuses to tell her a lie
The mirror won't let her simply pass by
Sun struck exposure, full moon bearing down
Where once was a smile lies a permanent frown

Take her here, take her there, take her anywhere
Away from the loss that a woman must bear
While his wrinkles are honored and with only one tooth
He knows not a mirror that will tell *him* the truth

ACKNOWLEDGMENTS

As time goes on, I will always think kindly of the people who have added magic and inspiration to my writing. There are so many to thank.

Robert Alan Radmer - the angel in my life who has been by my side throughout my publishing experience.

Don Tassone – my writing buddy, a marvelous author whose friendship and knowledge I treasure.

Kelly Holstine – an inspiration who followed her dream and opened Wordhaven BookHouse, a delightful independent bookstore in my favorite Midwest town, Sheboygan, Wisconsin. How delighted I am to have my books on your shelves.

The Alliance of Independent Authors and Indie writers all across the world – Bravo!

Kelsey Huse – beta reader extraordinaire, you're the best!

Friends and family, and the cool readers and authors I've met along this wonderful and challenging literary trail.

A big thanks to all who made my third book launch a huge success!

ABOUT THE AUTHOR

Libby Belle has shared that she's a mother of six, boasting eleven grandchildren, and has lived a full, rewarding life. What she hasn't shared with her readers is her fantasy.

"I have a deep desire to turn my stories into movies, driven by a lifelong fantasy of creating with the likes of directors, John Hughes and Peter Bogdanovich crammed in a small writer's room with no ceiling at a big round table rubbing elbows with these incredible talents – John Candy, Billy Crystal, Tim Conway, Gilda Radner, Dana Carvey, Madeline Kahn, Carol Burnett, and Robin Williams on a leash. I'd gladly make room for Tom Papa and Jim Gaffigan, and the writers for the 80's sitcom, *Wonder Years*. I still believe in the corny cliché – it's never too late to follow your dreams. I hope you do, too."

LibbyBelle.com

facebook.com/LibbyBelleStories

Other Books by Libby Belle

LibbyBelle.com
facebook.com/LibbyBelleStories

Made in the USA
Coppell, TX
16 September 2022

83251550R00148